WEEP NOT FOR ME

By

GARY COHEN

and

CATHERINE RUNYON

MOODY PRESS

CHICAGO

Copyright © 1980 by
THE MOODY BIBLE INSTITUTE
OF CHICAGO

Library of Congress Cataloging in Publication Data

Cohen, Gary G.
    Weep not for me.
    1. Jerusalem—Siege, A.D. 70—Fiction.
I. Runyon, Catherine, 1947- joint author. II. Title.
PZ4.C67696We   [PS3553.0423]   813'.54   80-10773
ISBN 0-8024-4309-5

Second Printing, 1981

Printed in the United States of America

Why was the Second Temple destroyed? Because of blind hatred.

The Talmud: Yoma 9b

JERUSALEM 66 A.D.

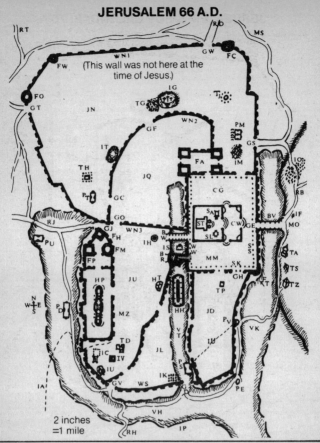

(This wall was not here at the time of Jesus.)

2 inches = 1 mile

Jerusalem

J - Jerusalem
JD David's city
JL Lower city
JU Upper city
JQ Quarter, second
JN New city

V - Valleys
VK Kidron
VH Hinnom
VT Tyropoean

G - Gates
GT Tower
GW Women's
GS Stephen's
GE East
GD Dung
GV Valley

GJ Joppa
GO Old
GC Corner
GF Fish
GH Hulda

R - Roads
RT Tyre
RD Damascus
RB Bethany
RH Hebron
RJ Joppa

T - Tombs
TH Hyrcanus
TJ Jannaeus
TG Garden
TA Absalom
TS Seir's sons

TZ Zechariah
TP Prophetess
TD David

W - Walls
WN1 North 1st
WN2 North 2nd
WN3 North 3rd
WS South
WW Wailing

B - Bridges
BV Valley
BW Wilson's
BR Robinson's- (Great Stairs)

H - Herod's
HP Palace

HT Theater
HH Hypodrome

S - Sacred
ST Temple
SA Altar
SL Laver
SS Solomon's porch
SK King's porch

C - Courts
CG Gentiles'
CW Women's

M - Mounts
MS Scopus
MO Olivet
MM Moriah
MZ Zion

JERUSALEM SIEGE CALENDAR, 70 A.D.

Camps of 15th & 12th Legions

(This wall was not here at the time of Jesus.)

Camp of 10th Legion

Camp of 5th Legion

2 inches = 1 mile

-gary g. cohen©

P - Pools
- **PT** Tower
- **PM** Market, sheep
- **PV** Virgin's
- **PE** En-rogel
- **PS** Siloam
- **PD** Dragon's
- **PU** Upper

F - Fortification Towers
- **FO** Octagonal (persiphanus)
- **FW** Women's
- **FC** Corner
- **FA** Antonia (praetorium)
- **FT** Temple (the pterugion)
- **FP** Phaesel
- **FH** Hippicus
- **FM** Mariame

I - Interest Points
- **IG** Gordon's calvary
- **IT** Traditional calvary
- **IM** Market, sheep
- **IO** Olive-press garden (gethsemene)
- **IS** Sanhedrin (between bridges)
- **IA** Underground water tunnel

- **IU** Upper room (traditional site)
- **IC** Caiaphas' palace
- **IK** King's garden
- **IH** Hasmonean palace
- **IP** Potter's field area
- **IF** Fig tree site, the cursed
- **IV** Villa of Matthias

THE SIEGE:
1. Day 15, Outer Wall.
2. Day 24, Middle Wall.
3. Day 73, Antonia Castle.
4. Day 95, Cloister Bldgs.
5. Day 107, Temple burns.
6. Day 109, Lower & David's Cities.
7. Day 139, Upper City falls.

PREFACE

No doubt for years you have heard about the Fall of Jerusalem 1,910 years ago. You have read articles here and there which mentioned how awful was the collapse of Jerusalem and how great was the suffering within, before the Romans broke through. Now, by means of the following historical novel, you may live and experience the tragic chain of events that led to the final destruction of the Holy City. As unfortunate events pile up one after another you will feel for yourself something of what it must have been like being dragged deeper and deeper into the Roman-Zealot feud. Perhaps for the first time you will mingle a tear of your own with those of the Jerusalem women to whom the cross-laden Jesus said,

> Daughters of Jerusalem, weep not for me, but weep for yourselves, and for your children. For, behold, the days are coming, in the which they shall say, Blessed are the barren, and the wombs that never bare, and the paps which never gave suck. [Luke 23:28-29]

The authors wish to acknowledge that in dealing with a topic so highly charged in emotion—involving religions, nations, barbarity, patriotism, and treason—not everyone will interpret these events as we have. If any person or group is in any way offended, our deepest apologies are offered.

Be assured that every attempt has been made to secure absolute historical accuracy. Even seemingly inconsequential events within the story—for example, an argument over a bird in Caesarea, or General Titus becoming angered at a Roman soldier who allowed his horse to be stolen—are based on factual documentation. Dates, place names, names of generals and legions, and locations in Jerusalem are accurate. One who reads this story will learn the basic facts of the history of this era—so vital to both Christians and Jews.

Special thanks go to the eyewitness, Flavius Josephus (*Wars of the Jews* [Phila.: Winston, 1957 ed.]); to Y. Aharoni and M. Avi-Yonah (*Macmillan Bible Atlas* [Jerusalem: Carta, 1968]); to the editors and authors of the *Encyclopaedia Judaica;* and to the authors of the Talmud.

With the very existence of the nation of Israel again threatened by a growing cloud of enemies, the message of this book takes on deep significance. May the God of the Bible save Israel! Come now, let us travel to the Holy Land two thousand years ago—Romans, Christians, and Jews move among the camels in the streets—let us laugh and weep with them!

1

The bronzed manservant came running up the hill to the olive grove where Joseph Matthias and his father worked, shouting as he came.

"My lord, my lord, they have stolen the oil and the lamps! What shall we do? They have taken everything."

He came stumbling, winded, afraid. The elder Matthias scowled. "Whatever is this news, Ahben, that you forget yourself in such a manner?"

The wealthy man felt that he knew what the news would be. If all were well, the caravan leader before him would be halfway to Joppa instead of here in his Jerusalem olive yards. Brigands, thieves, seemed the most likely interpretation of this preposterous approach, but the man before him was uninjured and fully clothed, not the usual product of an attack by highwaymen.

For a moment Matthias was angry as he glimpsed a band of Roman soldiers passing outside the gate. Where had they been when someone was stealing his precious oil? Probably sitting comfortably at the table of some unwilling Jewish host. So many years those soldiers had been a part of the familiar Jerusalem scenery, and still he had trouble accepting them.

The young man had halted and, after breathing deeply for a few moments, managed a deep bow. "Peace to you and your household, Matthias ben Joseph. I come with a message from Jabin, captain of your Joppa caravan. My lord, the Roman general quartered in Jerusalem, Mitelius by name, has taken all the oil and lamps."

The younger Matthias started in surprise. "Mitelius took

it! Why? He has purchased oil from us on many occasions. Was there trouble? Did you resist?"

Ahben shook his head. "We were well onto the plain when the small guard overtook us. They handled the captain roughly, but did him no harm. Mitelius himself led the investigation. He declared that our shipment was bound for the rebel Jews hiding in the hills, those who sometimes raid the Roman camps. The general said to tell you, since you are a respected citizen and have not been known to engage in rebel activity before, that he would say nothing to the governor but that of course he must confiscate the oil shipment himself."

"Of course," muttered Matthias bitterly. "Joseph, what do you make of this ridiculous story?"

"Make of it, Father? It's quite obvious. Mitelius cannot support his lavish way of life on a soldier's pay. Of course he would say nothing to the governor, since the seizure is illegal. Tomorrow, we could go to find the oil at the market, where Mitelius will have the peasants selling it for him." Though he was outraged, he could not dispel a small feeling of admiration for the general. A very resourceful man!

He envied the military leader. Though Joseph was the son of a rich merchant, the eldest in a respected family, knowledgeable, a leader in his own right, no Jew had any real power as long as Rome occupied the land. Everything had to be done carefully, with deference to the conqueror.

The prospect of simply walking into a situation and taking over excited him. It was not the way of his father or his aged uncle, wily Jews who dickered and circled in the way of their fathers. Joseph felt ashamed as he saw the look of concern on his father's face. Matthias would be deeply hurt if he fully understood the influence of the Romans on his son.

"I refuse to buy back my own oil," Matthias said with determination. "There must be some other way. Perhaps

I could talk to him, prove to him that I have no connection with those foolish hill people—"

"Father, Mitelius knows that. He knows you. It was only an excuse to take the oil, don't you see? He simply stole the oil, and he can do it because he is a Roman."

"Then we must report such misconduct to the governor."

"The governor is a thief as well. Besides, Mitelius is a general. Gessius Florus would never entertain a complaint against him. He would be afraid of a military rebellion."

The two men walked slowly toward their upper-Jerusalem home. "You are wise in the ways of Rome, my son. Sometimes, I fear you are too wise."

"One must be wise to live, Father."

"Does not the Lord keep His own? Guile is not His way."

"Nor mine. I speak only honest words to Roman or Jew."

"But sometimes the words have two meanings. I am old, Joseph, but I am neither blind nor deaf. I fear your friendship with Rome."

Joseph was irritated. "If that is true, why did you send me to visit the city? I was younger then. Were you not afraid of the influence of the heathen?"

"I had hoped that, seeing Caesar in his debauchery, witnessing firsthand his hatred for Jews, you might reaffirm your commitment to the paths of the Lord."

"Father, I follow the Law as carefully as you do."

His father smiled and said quietly. "But not with your heart. Do you? Can you tell me I am wrong?" His son hesitated, and the father's smile broadened. He chuckled. "No, I think not. And that is my fault, I suppose."

"No, Father. Please—" Joseph had no desire to hurt his father, and he searched for the right words. "Please be patient. Lately, many things cause me to doubt—your ways, and my own. I am unsure."

11

Once inside the city, they made their way to the Temple to participate in the evening sacrifice, then hurried home, tired and hungry.

"So late, my husband," said Sarah, frowning. "Something is wrong!"

"The Romans have stolen the entire shipment we sent to Joppa today. The caravan was barely out of the city when Mitelius halted it and took the oil and the lamps, too."

David ben Asher, Sarah's brother, rose from his seat like a thundercloud mounting in the sky. "Stolen! The ways of the wicked are a continual stench in the nostrils of the Almighty," he shouted.

"Quietly, Uncle," warned Joseph. "You might be heard."

"I care nothing for my life if it must be lived under the heels of heathens." He raised his fist toward the open window. "Every day I pray for the wrath of God to smite them."

"Ben Asher," said Matthias, shaking his head in mock sadness. "So old, and yet so rebellious? Can you not live and let live?" He saw the color rising in his brother-in-law's face and smiled obviously to let him know he had meant the remark to be sarcastic. "I know, David. I understand your indignation, but it does not help us get our oil back. Have you any ideas beyond overthrowing the Romans and expelling them from all Judea?"

David ben Asher calmed slightly but continued to stalk about the room. "I have none. I cannot think well when Romans are involved. Ask your son," he said bluntly. "He seems skillful in such matters."

Joseph stared rudely at his uncle, who paid no attention.

"What do you think, Joseph? Should we go to Mitelius?"

Joseph shook his head. "No, it would be pointless. I am sure the oil is gone by now. But I believe we might be paid for it, if we were to petition Gessius Florus in the right way."

12

"Beg that Gentile dog for favors? Never!" cried Uncle David.

"David, David, we are not so wealthy that we can simply forget an entire shipment of oil! We must try. What do you have in mind, Joseph?"

Joseph had hoped for this opportunity, and he tried not to sound too anxious. "Let me go to Caesarea, Father. I can speak to Gessius Florus. I've heard he is a lonely man, and given to pleasure. He can be turned, I believe."

His father eyed him carefully. "And you would be the one to do it, my son." He sighed. "Ah, what's the use? We are what we are. Go, use your 'talents.' I suppose it is not wrong to take from heathen what rightfully belongs to us."

"Thank you, Father! I shall leave tomorrow—with your permission."

"Yes, tomorrow. And Uncle David will go with you."

"Father! I can go—"

"Matthias! I can't go—"

"You can both go. I have decided. You will be good for each other."

The evening meal was somewhat sullen. The women carried food in and out, Sarah serving her husband, and Miriam, Joseph's intended bride, serving him and Uncle David. He accepted her service without thanks, almost without notice. Lately she seemed to be busy more and more with his mother, and they spent little time together. Tonight his thoughts were even further away as he remembered the events of the day and contemplated his trip.

Caesarea! He had not been away from Jerusalem in some time, and the prospects of being in the busy port city brought a smile to his face.

"Oh! I was thinking of other things, Miriam."

She nodded and smiled, and Joseph felt guilty, knowing that she assumed he was thinking of her, of their marriage.

13

Well, it would do no harm to let her think what she wanted. Her world held few enough joys, it seemed to him. Yet she appeared happy, and he was grateful for that. She really was quite lovely, even serene. The marriage would be good for him, and for the family. She would be a good helper.

He went to his room early, knowing that they would rise long before daylight to begin the trip to Caesarea. He stood and looked out at the night sky, thinking of the great God that infiltrated his life at every point—eating, washing, working, family—they were all based on the laws of Jehovah and were practiced so incessantly from youth that he had forgotten they were laws, and not necessarily a natural part of his being. "Hear, O Israel, the Lord our God is one Lord. . . ." So different, he thought, from the gods of the Romans, who seemed to worship everything, including the emperor. Joseph trembled at the thought. Apparently Jehovah had no interest in them. He chastised His own people severely for such a transgression, but the Romans prospered. Truly, the ways of God were strange. And Joseph knew that any venture begun must have the blessing of God to succeed. He had no doubts about Jehovah; He was unchanging, austere, demanding, and precise. To the best of his ability, Joseph conformed to His commands—*But not with your heart.* His father's words echoed in his mind. A strange emptiness engulfed him, and he wondered if he had ever done anything with all his heart, for he seemed to be tugged in many directions all the time. He shrugged the feelings away and lay down. For now, he had one goal—to win back his father's investment, and something inside him, perhaps his heart, warmed to the challenge.

2

Gessius Florus sat heavily on his bench in the alabaster Hall of the Procurator. Dressed in an expensive senatorial brown toga, he was visibly dejected. His excess weight drooped on his short frame on this sweltering afternoon.

He looked about the solid stone hall and shook his head in disgust at the whiteness everywhere in view—white walls, white ceiling, white benches, and white statues!

No variety. No taste, he thought, wishing that the costly Parian and Pentelic marble slabs could be replaced, if only for an instant, by the cool green pines of Rome along the Tiber. He sighed, feeling sorry for himself. His mind wandered back to the worrisome fears that had been haunting him for the last few months.

Albinus, his predecessor, had lasted only two years. Gessius himself had served almost two years as procurator, but he still had not saved enough money for retirement in Rome. *And these Jews drive me insane every day with their petty complaints,* he thought. Judea was not kind to Roman governors. Then, too, the troublesome Christians were secretly spreading their poison even in Caesarea, in spite of Nero Caesar's ban. *I must accept it,* he mused, *I am not as young as I used to be, and I cannot take this kind of life much longer. Something must change.* Somehow, there had to be more money, less tension, fewer incidents. If he could make a name for himself in Judea, his future would be secure, and perhaps he might even gain a place in history. He contemplated the possibilities—firmer discipline among the Jews, more favors, more soldiers— until an expected voice interrupted him.

"Your Excellency," the mellow male voice called from the back of the hall. "It is the eighth hour. Shall I admit the people?" It was Epaenetus, the prefect in charge of the general administration, dutifully making his daily plea to begin the afternoon's hearing.

Gessius' short white beard bristled and sparkled with perspiration in the midafternoon heat. He forced a more cheerful look to his face as he prepared to meet the entering petitioners. Still his mind started to wander, and he began to think of Octavia, his attractive young wife, and to wonder what she might order for his evening meal.

She was tall and slender, typical of the dark-haired, olive-skinned beauties who came from the town of Perugia north of Rome. Octavia! Yes, he must put more money aside, a good deal of money. He had no misconceptions about his marriage. What had an old, fat, balding Roman like himself to offer such a beauty? Once the status of procurator's wife was changed, she might look elsewhere. He must work carefully these days. Former procurators had not distinguished themselves—at least not positively—in this wretched land.

Gessius was brought back to his immediate situation with a start as hosts of people began to pour into the Hall of the Procurator. Six stately Roman centurions led the way, helmets in hand, marching up the aisle with their red capes flowing and their bronze breastplates glistening. The centurions marched in step, a pair walking shoulder to shoulder up each of the three aisles amid the ranks of white marble benches.

Then without warning two trumpets sounded from the rear. To the stranger it was an awesome show, but Gessius grimaced and all but put his fingers to his ears as the piercing notes reverberated against the marble walls, floors, and ceilings. How he hated that moment! Yet it was an unavoidable part of pomp necessary to a Roman court, and he

16

feared that if he dispensed with it someone might report him to Rome.

The prefect's voice, now loud and bold, cried the ritualistic greeting of the Roman court. "All remain standing for the Procurator of Judea, Samaria, Lower Galilee, and Western Gilead, His Excellency Gessius Florus, Citizen of Rome and member of the Equestrian Order, Procurator by the will of Nero Caesar, Pontifex Maximus."

Before him stood an assorted mixture of humanity—Greeks and Romans from the west, Parthians from the east, and Syrians and Jews from Palestine itself. At last, because of the colors of the tunics, robes, and turbans of those present, the empty whiteness of the hall was given life and variety. Gessius was pleased, and he nodded to the prefect, signaling that the people might now be seated. The imperial provincial court was now in session.

Gessius smiled broadly at the people. The smile said to all that the procurator, despite the many tales of his injustices and thieveries, apparently desired to be friendly and wished his subjects to be affably disposed toward himself. Everyone in the courtroom seemed to understand, and instantly the sunny, broad grin of Gessius had transformed the stern stone hall into a dazzle of human smiles.

"First case," demanded Gessius. His grin abruptly vanished, and the somber preoccupied face reappeared. The assembly was reminded that the figure before them held the power of life and death, and with his word went freedom or the endless toil of the galleys—or worse.

Joseph Matthias, in attendance with his aging uncle, was very much aware of the mood of the procurator. The keen businessman's eye did not miss the ruler's cultivated taste for luxury, the moody stare, the obvious boredom.

"This Gessius is a man to be catered to," he muttered to the stately old man at his side. He whispered in Hebrew,

17

lifting his head a little to speak into the tall old uncle's ear. "He loves flattery. See how he enjoys frightening the people? Just wait. See how I turn the power of Rome to our advantage."

Uncle David ben Asher said nothing, but he was definitely upset with his nephew. The young these days did not seem to understand that using Rome was not the issue, that surviving was not the real goal. To be rid of Rome completely was the greatest dream.

They listened as a servile-looking scribe, very thin, apparently about eighty years old, rose and read from a papyrus: "Baruch ben Mordechai, Jew of the city of Joppa, accused of stealing a sword from a Roman soldier, Gaius Paullus."

Almost an hour went by as the procurator and various Roman officials questioned the accused, a frightened, dark-haired, nineteen-year-old Jewish boy. Uncle David closed his eyes and raised his hands ever so slightly. He prayed on behalf of the boy in a low voice. "O God, the proud are risen against me, and the assemblies of violent men have sought after my soul. . . . But thou, O Lord, art a God full of compassion, and gracious, longsuffering, and plenteous in mercy and truth. O turn unto me, and have mercy upon me; give thy strength unto thy servant, and save the son of thine handmaid. Shew me a token for good; that they which hate me may see it, and be ashamed."*

After almost an hour of accusations and arguments, the father of the accused prostrated himself before the procurator, sobbing in frustration and fear.

"Spare him, I beg you," the man implored. "He is my only son. I will repay a thousand times what the sword is worth. Please, decide in our favor. But decide—soon!"

Gessius's badgering and delays had brought results, as usual. He leaned forward and whispered to the sobbing

*Psalm 86:14-17.

father, "Could you raise the sum of twenty silver shekels?"

The father eagerly nodded and exclaimed, "Gladly! I have possessions that can be sold."

Gessius now motioned with his left hand to the prefect that he was ready to give the verdict, and the prefect called everyone to an immediate silence. Debate among the spectators ceased. All waited to see who had won.

Gessius assumed a fatherly bearing, and he began to speak slowly and deliberately, weighing every word.

"There is much confusion over what precisely occurred here. Everyone admits that it was dark in Joppa on the night of this event. It appears to me that what really happened was that the boy accidentally bumped the soldier, who was somehow distracted from his watch. The sword dropped, the boy picked it up, saw the look on Paullus' face, became frightened, and ran with the sword."

The father was noticeably relieved, as was the soldier. Gessius continued, "I free the boy with a warning—there is plenty of room in Roman ships. And I pronounce that you, Paullus, are likewise innocent of any shirking of duty, and that you may return to your unit without shame or punishment."

"Thanks be unto the Eternal One," sobbed the father, bowing again before the procurator. Uncle David echoed his thanks but was uneasy over the credit being given Gessius Florus. From back in the hall, a woman, the boy's mother, shouted aloud in broken Greek, "May the God of my people bless you, O noble procurator!" Uncle David cringed.

Gessius was pleased at this spontaneous cry of appreciation. He therefore, with a wave of his hand, signaled a rising centurion not to rebuke the woman for shouting out in the court. Gessius leaned back, adjusting his regal brown robe, and made no attempt to hold back the smile of satisfaction that went across his wide face. A small but definite gesture to the elated old Jew before him sent the man scurrying to a private conversation with Gessius' treasurer.

The gesture was not missed by Joseph Matthias, nor did its interpretation escape him. He quickly reviewed his own defense in the light of his observations, as the prefect announced their case.

"The house of Matthias petitions the procurator for payment of 136 silver denarii for 120 barrels of olive oil taken by the Roman garrison at Jerusalem and for sixteen barrels of pottery lamps seized by the same."

Young Joseph and his uncle came forward. They were dressed in white linen levitical garb, with blue sashes around their waists and turbans upon their heads. They courteously removed the turbans as they bowed before the procurator, Uncle David showing obvious reluctance.

"I am Joseph Matthias," the younger man announced. "I am the son of Matthias ben Joseph, an important and wealthy oil and pottery merchant of Jerusalem."

The words were not wasted. Gessius was immediately interested. This man spoke the common Greek well, a blessing after the hours of sifting through thick country accents.

Joseph presented the large, surly man beside him. "This is my uncle, David ben Asher of the tribe of Levi, brother-in-law to my father."

An old one, thought Gessius, *orthodox, fanatical.* Their eyes met and they knew this would be their only communication. David ben Asher refused the Greek language, and Gessius knew no Hebrew apart from the curses he had learned to recognize and a few business terms.

He allowed the latent animosity to remain unchallenged and turned to Joseph. "Tell me how the garrison came to obtain your oil and lamps in the first place."

"Your Excellency, your esteemed general in Jerusalem, General Mitelius, confiscated the 136 barrels from my father's camel caravan because he thought that we were

20

smuggling oil and weapons to the Zealots hiding in the north. It was, however, just a routine delivery going out to Joppa. My father's house is innocent.

"Be assured that our sympathies do not lie with the enemies of Rome. We want peace in Jerusalem. A quiet society is to our advantage—and yours." A subtle change came to his face, a tilt of the head, a movement of the eyes. "As we prosper, so you prosper."

"I see," Gessius said slowly, studying the young man. He held Joseph's steady gaze for a moment until he was sure he had interpreted the remark correctly. Then he leaned forward and asked with deliberate harshness, "Why did your father not come and explain all of this to me in person? Does he spurn the Roman court?"

"My father is a busy merchant," Joseph said, humility in his voice. "He is master of a large household, which would suffer from his absence. If he does not make money, how can he pay his taxes? Besides, he felt that since I had traveled to Rome and can read and write Latin as well as Greek, I would represent him well. Of course, my father is wiser than I and he would have stated the case much—"

"You visited Rome?" Gessius exclaimed.

"Yes, two and a half years ago, before the great fire. There I became acquainted with Aliturius the actor, and through him met Poppea, wife of Caesar."

"You were there before the terrible fire, were you? And you say that you were acquainted with Poppea!" Then, in more cautious tones, "Tell me the truth now, Hebrew. If you just said this to win your case, I will not punish you at all." He paused, then added, "We shall just consider your case lost, and you may leave without saying another word. You see, my wife knows Poppea well."

Joseph remained calm, with a look of gentle hurt at the mistrust of the procurator. "O excellent procurator, rest assured that my story is true." He began to speak in Latin,

21

describing Poppea, the theater in Rome, the sights and entertainments he had enjoyed. "How I enjoyed Rome. How you must miss the beautiful seven hills—Capitoline, Palatine, Aventine, Quirinal—"

"Enough," stated the now smiling procurator. "You make me homesick. It is good to hear Latin again. You have brightened my day, young man. Obviously, you are telling the truth, for whatever motive. How can I deny restitution to a family who, ah—supports Rome. You stated the value of the shipment at 136 denarii?" Joseph nodded, and Gessius rubbed his chin thoughtfully. "Still, it is difficult to contradict the judgment of one's own general."

Joseph spoke quickly. "I will explain to my father that the difference of fifteen denarii was compensation for wages to the military witnesses who supported our case. They are here, are they not?"

"Uh—yes. Of course. Their testimony was recorded earlier by the scribe. Of course, I remember. They substantiated your claim completely. Simply a precautionary measure on the part of General Mitelius—understandable in these times."

Gessius looked at Joseph for agreement and approval. Joseph nodded and smiled, but somehow felt ashamed of his pandering. He was thankful that Uncle David, who did not know the meaning of the word *compromise,* did not understand the Roman games being played. Had he become too friendly with this great man? By enjoying the companionship of one who could talk with him about his marvelous trip to Rome, had he perhaps tacitly given the impression that he accepted the atrocities and oppression of the Roman occupation? Would those in the court view him as a traitor instead of as a shrewd businessman? He pronounced a silent reproach to himself. It did not matter what others thought. *Me first,* he reminded himself. *We must live the best way we can.*

22

"Fortuna favet fortibus," Gessius said in dismissal to Joseph, and as a reassurance to himself. "Fortune favors the bold."

The two men turned to the treasurer and waited for their reimbursement. But before they could leave the hall, a flurry of activity at the back of the courtroom caught everyone's attention and sent the prefect scurrying for a conference with the centurions. Soon he returned and spoke to the procurator in hushed tones.

"Excellency, there has been a fight. It seems some Greek boys killed a bird in front of the synagogue. The Jews there took it as an insult, a mocking of their sacrifice. A street fight resulted. The officers have arrested as many participants as possible and brought them here for immediate judgment. Perhaps, Excellency, if an example were to be made—?"

"I know my job, prefect. I will hear the case."

The soldiers presented themselves and the scruffy group of fighters before the procurator and began the accusations. The audience was immediately divided, Greek against Jew, Jew against Roman, as the various accounts of the incident were related.

Gessius was sensitive to the mounting tension. How he hated these religious disputes! No matter what he decided, no one would be happy.

David and Joseph waited for the decision so that they could take the news home to Jerusalem. But suddenly the trivial street fight was given new significance.

Uncle David tugged excitedly at Joseph's sleeve. "Joseph! Joseph! There will be trouble." He pointed past the crowd to an open window where a group of men could be seen approaching the entrance.

A delegation of about a dozen Jewish elders, headed by the aged, white-haired John ben Shlomo, boldly entered and came marching up the center aisle of the marbled Roman hall. Their white robes and turbans—so different from the multicolored clothes of the crowd—seemed to rival even the white hall in brilliance.

All eyes turned in shock upon these who so arrogantly and boldly barged into the procurator's presence. Gessius was instantly angry, but his response was lost on the determined men who moved deliberately toward him.

John ben Shlomo stared contemptuously at Gessius Florus until the entire group had reached the front of the hall. Arrogantly they elbowed their way into the group of prisoners from the street fight and past the guards until they stood directly in front of the procurator, heads high, mouths set. Hatred burned between the two leaders, a tangible wave in the already oppressive heat.

Joseph frowned, uneasy in the explosive situation. *Don't look haughty and demanding at this Roman, or it is you who will soon be humbled,* he thought as he looked at John ben Shlomo. The look on Uncle David's face was one of pure admiration for the leader who would put the Gentiles in their place. There was a subtle movement of the uncle's hands, and Joseph knew that he was again praying. Joseph did not have to wonder for whom Uncle David asked blessings.

John ben Shlomo spoke: "O procurator, you have already heard of this latest fight between our Jewish men and these ruffian Greeks. These men with me represent the Jewish community of Caesarea, some twenty thousand souls. We wish to remind you that not long ago we paid you the huge sum of eight silver talents for the assurance of your protection, and you have still failed to live up to your part of the agreement." The cold, aristocratic tones became charged with emotion as John ben Shlomo described the alleged sacrilege and violence at the synagogue.

As he droned on it became obvious to everyone in the great hall, except the austere group in white, that the rabbi

24

had exceeded his bounds. The procurator's anger was more and more apparent, and a nervous silence fell on the crowd.

"We demand the protection that you promised and for which we have paid you. Furthermore, we have removed our sacred scrolls of the Torah to the town of Narbata. And when our high priest asks us why, we shall have to answer that we removed them from Caesarea either because the procurator *would not* make good his pledge of protection to us, for which we paid dearly, or because he was *unable* to make good his pledge of protection to us, in which case—"

Gessius Florus jumped to his feet, enraged, and shouted, "Will you take the procurator of Judea to task publicly for his actions, you vile Jew?" He stepped menacingly forward and leaned into the face of John ben Shlomo. "It is you who breaks your word and our agreement! Who gave you permission to remove valuable scrolls from the city of the procurator?"

"The point is—"

"They are treasures, are they not? And you know very well that it is unlawful for non-Romans to remove treasures from Caesarea?"

"But the fighting, we—"

"Centurion! Hold these Jews for a later hearing on the charge of unlawfully removing treasures from Caesarea. Now get them out of my sight."

"Gessius Florus, we have more—"

"No, I will hear no more!" he shouted. He turned his back as the guards dragged the humiliated, protesting Jews from the hall.

Joseph shook his head. The old ones who would not bend! Was there any hope for them at all? Uncle David sagged noticeably and studied the floor. Where was Jehovah?

Gessius Florus called for the prefect. With a wry smile,

he officially pronounced a penalty. "I am today levying a fine of seventeen gold talents upon the Temple treasury in Jerusalem. This fine is to repay Caesar for the treasures unlawfully snatched out of Caesarea by Jewish leaders and spirited away to Narbata. Send word to Ananias, the old high priest in charge of the treasury, to have the money ready by the second day of next week. At that time I will come to Jerusalem with soldiers to receive it for Caesar."

"Yes, my procurator," was the elderly prefect's curt reply as he crossed his right arm over his breastplate in a hurried salute. Instantly he turned around and rushed to dispatch a messenger to Jerusalem with the latest demand.

"No more cases today," added the angry and weary procurator, wrinkling his forehead as he glanced from the prefect to the startled crowd. "See if you can't settle some of the lesser disputes without me."

Throughout the incident, Joseph had been giving his uncle a running interpretation. The old man was dismayed and desperately saddened by the affair, and Joseph was sorry that he could not help. For a moment, Joseph envied him for his commitment, his absolute sense of right.

Gessius stopped and spoke to them as he left the judgment bench for his private quarters. "You don't approve of my actions, do you? No, I can tell by your faces. You Jews do stick together. And you, fat one, you hate me. Ha! You are even fatter than I! I like you for that." David ben Asher stood mute before the unintelligible onslaught. "Do take notice that I was merciful in putting the fine on the Temple treasuries rather than on those thirteen who tried to humiliate me publicly. If I had fined them personally, they would all have been sold to the galleys before they could have raised the necessary gold. They must learn their lesson. It is Rome which rules, and not these ancient priests." He looked directly into Joseph's eyes. "Your countrymen would do well to follow your example, and not mix business and politics with religion."

The hall cleared, and Joseph and David mingled with the outgoing crowd.

"John ben Shlomo is a truly righteous man," Uncle David declared, his spirit lifting at the thought of such a hero. "He had no fear. He demanded justice. Did you hear him?"

"Do you know where he is now?" Joseph interrupted angrily. "Do you know that he only escaped death because of Gessius's desire to avoid stirring up the Jews, for his own benefit? Uncle, don't you see that the old fool and his ridiculous principles brought us a step closer to war today? I wish Gessius had demanded personal payment. Why should the people be taxed for John ben Shlomo's arrogance?"

"Joseph, he is an elder. Do you not fear God?"

"I fear God, Uncle. And I fear Rome. And right now, I cannot say which I fear more."

They passed the synagogue where the mock sacrifices had taken place. The scene was quiet. Roman guards were stationed every few meters, wary, alert.

Uncle David paused, deep in thought. At last he turned to Joseph and spoke solemnly.

"Sometimes I wonder if I will ever see peace. Do you know that in my whole lifetime so far there has never been peace for my people—your people, Joseph? The peace of Rome, that is not peace. When wicked Gentiles make light of the God of our fathers and of His laws, where is peace? Joseph," the big old man looked down at his nephew, tenderness filling his voice, "I am sad. Almost, I lose hope."

3

"What can we tell the women?" Joseph asked. He and his somber uncle dismounted from their sweating Arabian horses for a break in their trek home. They had left Caesarea early and headed eastward down the old Joppa road, hoping to reach Jerusalem before the midday heat made traveling unbearable.

"We must tell them the truth, Joseph."

"And alarm them into thinking that war with Rome is ahead?" Joseph retorted, somewhat irritated at the simplistic and seemingly unfeeling answer the surly old bear had given.

"They will learn it sooner or later, Joseph. It is in the wind. And before we get home the messenger from the procurator will arrive with his news of the Temple tax. Our women will know the news before the men, no doubt."

The two men sat in silence to eat some dried figs and drink a little water. Joseph thought of Miriam, imagined her going to the well with the other women and hearing of the Temple tax. Would she understand the significance? He doubted it. Somehow she failed to sense the political feeling in Judea. Of course, she was a woman; still, Joseph longed for a genuine companion in marriage, one who considered issues and times, who could compliment him intelligently instead of dutifully. He would have to spend more time with her and encourage her to listen and think.

With this in mind, he said to his uncle, "We must try to give the women hope. If the Moderates can continue to restrain the Zealot influence, we may yet avoid any real confrontation."

28

"All right, Joseph. But I shall tell no lies." David ben Asher squinted into the sun thoughtfully, and then spoke into the distance, away from his nephew. "I think there will be little hope among the men, least of all your father Matthias. Well he knows the power of the Zealot leaders, and you know what their reaction to the gold levy will be. They will want to retaliate instantly."

"Yes, I know. But perhaps for the sake of the women we can present it gently."

"This truth is as gentle as a knife. War and death may again come to our people."

The two men remounted and resumed their journey at a gallop. The sun rose to meet them as they raced toward the east, their seventy-mile trip almost complete.

Then, as their two mounts rose onto the crest of a small elevation in the road, it appeared before their eyes—Jerusalem, "beautiful for situation." High atop the plateau in the distance stood the wonderful City of David. Its pink-white limestone walls of ponderous cut stone appeared to be almost dark red in the distance as the ancient fortress stretched out on its sacred hill.

The Joppa gate pierced the middle of the wall just where the higher land of the north met the Hinnon Valley toward the south. Through this gate, pulled down and rebuilt, had passed the kings of Judah, the Maccabees, and the Galilean from Nazareth. Twenty towers at intervals interrupted the top of the horizontal line of the wall, and the sight once again gave Joseph and ben Asher a feeling of everlasting strength and serenity. *Jerusalem lives and will live* was the message of the massive walls. Safety, security, a city that could not be defeated—it was all there in the distance.

The highway soon became littered with an elongated camel caravan. It had originated from Jerusalem and was headed for the ships back at the port of Joppa. The clumsy animals seemed to pour out of the city gate and spill down the slopes onto the plain.

Joseph and Uncle David met men of the caravan and exchanged the elaborate greetings characteristic of travelers. Yes, the messenger from Caesarea had arrived just after nightfall the previous evening. No, the Sanhedrin had made no decision as yet, but it would certainly meet tonight.

Anxious now, David and Joseph hurried into the city. Once through the gate, they pushed southward through the narrow corridors of the upper city. The familiar smells of camels and donkeys, and of the tasty pastries and spoiled meats of a thousand shops, were everywhere. Here, a half mile south of the gate, was located the comfortable villa of Joseph's father. As the two travelers led their horses through the city, Joseph found himself wishing that all the pilgrims from the recent Passover would have left his city more promptly. The crowds had lingered for weeks, and it was still mobbed now in *Iyar* (May). Nevertheless, it was home and still beautiful to Joseph's troubled eyes.

The foreign faces around him meant little to Joseph. The children of Abraham were certainly his brothers, but the Jews native to Jerusalem were his true kinsmen. He had spent his entire life in this city, sometimes not going outside the walls for months at a time. All he had, all he loved, was here. The pilgrims came to worship at the Temple, and he could not disguise a faint air of superiority that it was his Temple, that they were outsiders whom he entertained.

As for Uncle David, the Temple was the city. Though Joseph believed in the God of his fathers and obeyed the commandments, belief and obedience were a way of life for his uncle. For David ben Asher, Jerusalem was more than home. It was a chosen city for chosen people, a symbol of an exclusive God.

The two men left the rabble for the more fashionable neighborhood of the Matthias family. As they entered the courtyard of the family villa, they saw Matthias ben Joseph waiting for them in the doorway. They embraced and entered the house together to discuss the trip and the news, and to eat and rest. The real activity of the day was yet to come.

* * *

The half-moon shone brightly as Matthias ben Joseph, his son, and his brother-in-law paced northward through a half mile of narrow streets in the upper city. Though the marts were closed, people hurried purposefully about the dark streets, a telltale sign of the suspense that hung in the air. The years of Roman occupation had been punctuated with "incidents." Messiahs rose and fell. Rome remained, all the while chafing at the constant harrassment from Jewish leaders. But a strike at the heart of Jerusalem, the Temple and its gold, raised emotions to fever pitch.

Against the light from the moon, to the left of the striding trio, rose the stern stone walls that enclosed the Herodian Palace, a Roman monument. On the right, just over the flat marts and rooftops with people sitting on them, stood the gray brown walls that separated the upper city from the more humble and rundown lower city to the southeast where the Pharisees lived in zealous pride.

Soon the three reached a wide marble staircase that led them down into the gaping jaws of the northern end of the city's central Cheesemaker's Valley and into the squat, gray-stoned Sanhedrin. A doorkeeper gave a knowing nod to Joseph's father and all three were permitted entrance. Already men were packed shoulder to shoulder inside. With the shutters closed for secrecy and a hundred oil lamps kindled, the comparatively small hall was like an oven and the men and priests within like so many white pottery figurines ready for baking. Joseph and ben Asher squatted on stools while Matthias went forward to take his regular seat.

Manahem, the bearded and unbridled youth, Zealot leader and spokesman, was already soaked with sweat from the emotional exertion of the night. "We must draw the line," he declared vehemently. "There is oppression at every hand. The Romans not only occupy our land and confiscate money in the form of taxes, which rightly belong to our God and our people, but they also encourage the other Palestinian Gentiles to persecute us. There is no punishment for these incidents—Jews are openly mocked—even stoned. We *can* stop them! We are a mighty nation still, with great resources, as Rome well knows. We must not be fooled into believing that Rome is invincible." He raised example after example of the vicious nature of the Roman army and of the corruption and immorality of the Roman governors. He ended by stating that immediate action was necessary in light of the monstrous tax imposed so unfairly by Gessius Florus.

Manahem's cohort, the priest Eleazar, was Manahem's opposite. Clean and clad in white, calculating and resourceful, he had only one thing in common with the crude, unkempt, vocal, and fiery Manahem—a passionate desire to rid Judea of the Romans. He reminded the people of the successful rebellion Judas the Maccabee had led against the oppressor Antiochus 230 years earlier. "If Judas Maccabaeus had waited for the approval of the Sanhedrin of his day," Eleazar said, "Israel would still be under the Syrians and a pagan statue would still pollute the holy Temple!"

The Zealots shouted unanimous approval, and the clamor between them and the Moderates lasted for several minutes before the high priest was able to restore order again.

Throughout the night, Joseph tried to assess each speaker, attempting to place his sympathies with one faction or the other. The Zealots confused him. Were they righteously indignant, or only selfish? Did they seek purity in Judea for the good of the people, or did they wish to become legends along with the hero Judas Maccabaeus? And the Moderates—were they cautious, or afraid? Was his father so taken with the improvements in trade brought about by Roman culture that he forgot his own national and religious heritage? And his own feelings—was he more like his uncle, or more like his father? Did he really want the Romans to leave, or would he be happy to use them peacefully throughout his adult life? Certainly he was repulsed by Manahem, but he was nervous about Eleazar. Was there no middle ground?

Rumor was abroad that the procurator feared an official investigation from Rome on the charges of corruption and embezzlement of imperial funds. The Moderates claimed further that he had been heard to remark jokingly that if a rebellion were to break out in Judea, all of those Jews who might testify against him in such an investigation would be conveniently killed. With this possibility in mind, Joseph's father and other wiser heads were able to persuade at least a few of the more rational among the group that they must not be provoked into a war, but that they must rather appeal to Caesar in Rome for the removal of Gessius.

"Perhaps my son Joseph might obtain an audience with Nero Caesar," Matthias volunteered. "If Caesar could understand that a competent, honest governor here would be an improvement—"

"No governor at all would be the only improvement," shouted a Zealot. "Tell him that when you go."

"I don't believe Caesar is in a mood to listen to Jews just now," Joseph said. "The followers of Jesus of Nazareth have been persecuted in Rome for some time. He believes that they are only a Jewish sect. He does not know our ways. Some say he is mad anyway."

"We must help ourselves," retorted the Zealot. "We must *not* pay the tax!"

"But we must," responded Matthias. "I prefer to placate Rome as long as money is the main issue. They leave us our lives and our laws and leaders. Did the Babylonians do as much?"

The debate raged throughout the night and through the early morning hours until nearly sunrise.

At last a final vote was taken and the result was announced by Ananus, son of Annas the high priest. "We shall pay the tax to Gessius Florus." Manahem, Eleazar, and their followers exploded. "Treason against Jewry! Treason!"

But the vote was done. The decision meant that there would be practically nothing left in the Temple treasury for any future arbitrary requisition. It was a shallow victory for the Moderates.

The people began to leave the hall, some angry, some sad, some relieved. The crowd edged through the streets, fatigue evident in every body. The day was just beginning, and hearts were already heavy.

* * *

At sunrise on the appointed second day of the week, an assemblage of over one hundred of these same people gathered along the Joppa road outside the western walls of the city to await the arrival of the procurator from Caesarea.

"It is Capito, the centurion, with a troop of about fifty soldiers." The message filtered back to Joseph as he stood beside his father.

Suddenly, amid the clatter of two hundred hooves, fifty Roman soldiers, a half-century unit, mounted a small rise. Their brass helmets and breastplates sparkled with the sun, and their scarlet plumes and capes, now hued with ochre dust from the ride, made them look resplendent with power.

Anticipating Gessius to be just around the bend in the road, the high priest was preparing to mouth his opening words of petition when the centurion took everyone by surprise by ordering, "Disperse!"

The priest stammered and no one moved.

"You heard me, Jews. Disperse at once! The procurator wants no conference outside the city. He will talk to you at one hour past noon in the North Court of the Herodian Palace, where he will be staying. Now disperse at once. The three hundred horseman who follow me will not share the road."

"Does he think the high priest of Israel is a dog to be spit at as he rides by?" shouted an outraged Uncle David. "Is Gessius so soft that he cannot sleep at the Praetorium, like the former procurators? Must he stay at the Herodian Palace, which doesn't even belong to him?"

"Who questions the procurator's order?" demanded the suddenly infuriated Capito. No one betrayed Uncle David or any of the others who had voiced their indignation. "Disperse, Jews," the commander repeated. "Do not provoke me further."

His words were soon muffled by the noise of the horses and trumpets of the three hundred Romans now accompanying Gessius down the road toward the Joppa Gate. So large a guard for even a procurator spelled only trouble for the city, and everyone in the crowd, as well as the Sadducees, ever loyal to the high priest, felt so outraged that when the procurator came into view, they began to hurl insults at him from amid the safe obscurity of the crowd.

"Threw the beggar a denarius," shouted someone at Gessius. In a moment, Gessius felt himself hit with a barrage of small coins as the entire mob tossed coins his way and chanted in unison, "Throw the beggar a coin! Throw the beggar a coin!"

The Roman guard passed on into the city, leaving the

35

angry, frustrated Jews standing in the road. They soon followed at a distance and entered the city in the dust of the entourage.

Thirty minutes later, in their upper-city home, Joseph's father stormed up and down within the lavish dining quarters. "The ignorant Zealots played right into Gessius's hands! We are fortunate that he did not stop his procession and order all of us butchered on the spot for the insults shouted at him. You mind me, Joseph: our people will pay dearly for publicly ridiculing the procurator."

Joseph replied, "Gessius is a reasonable man; he can be dealt with—at least, if there's money in the bargain for him. But you are right. We will suffer if those insane Zealots continue to insult him, or if one of the Sicarii knifes another Roman, as one did last month. Then we are destined to suffer, and we have destined it ourselves."

Uncle David shook his head from side to side. "I disagree with you, Joseph. The Romans are in our land, and have been for one hundred twenty-nine years now. Their procurator is demanding our holy Temple money. They are the ones to be blamed more than the Zealots. They heap wrong upon wrong."

"They are all to be blamed," said Matthias. "First, it is the Romans' fault because they are the intruders in our land. Second, Gessius the procurator is in the wrong for his abuses. But, my dear ones, the Zealots and Sicarii are also to blame because they continually goad the Romans by returning violence for violence."

Matthias continued with a proverb. "The Zealots are like a good little boy who throws a big stone at a bad dog that is barking at all the cihldren. When the dog is hit, he stops barking and bites and kills half the children. So, in the end, everyone was better off without the good boy who in righteousness threw the stone at the dog."

"Father is right as always," declared Joseph, rising from

his purple-cushioned Tiberian chair. "The Romans are the dogs, but the retaliation of the stupid Zealots will yet cause the Romans to destroy Jerusalem and kill us all."

"Joseph, it is the city of the Great King!" Uncle David said. "It is God's city. Such pronouncements are foolish."

Matthias said, "It has been done before, David. Prepare the house for battle—let's not be too secure. We shall trust the Lord, but we shall make plans as well. I believe the procurator has only delayed his revenge so that it might be more exacting."

Then, turning toward Joseph, Matthias continued, "My son, you will yet see another side of Gessius. He has given us our shipment, and you were wise in your ways, though I might wish you had been completely honest. But soon another side of his nature will reveal itself, and he will get from every Jew in Jerusalem, including us, more than gold. As for now, David and I will start collecting some of our accounts. We will settle for half or less if necessary. I have a feeling that soon we had better have all of our money nearby and a good set of camels to flee to Joppa."

The older men left the house, and Joseph watched them go out through the courtyard. He caught sight of the servants grinding near the house, and he saw Miriam collecting the flour to be taken to the kneading trough in the house and then to the baker.

He watched her movements and knew that she was thinking only of her work, learning all the ways of the Matthias household under the careful tutoring of her future mother-in-law.

As yet the dowry had not been paid to Miriam's widowed mother. The bethrothal ceremony had somehow been allowed to remain in the future, but there was no misunderstanding among the involved parties. Miriam and Joseph would marry. They had known each other for many years, the families were known and respected, the match had been understood almost from childhood. Miriam would be a good wife. She was devout, almost as devout as Uncle David, but even that thought nagged at Joseph. He knew that Uncle David believed all the traditions because they were good and right, in his own estimation. But Miriam, he knew, believed because she had considered no alternative. But of course, the end result was the same. And what did it matter?

It mattered. Joseph could not fool himself. He was old enough now to catch the silent communication between his parents, the knowing looks, the understood pauses. They were of one mind. And he also understood that though his mother said little, as was the custom, she was often the one who made decisions. And when she knew she was right, no amount of threatening and no number of promises from her husband could move her. In the business, she never interfered. But in matters of judgment and human nature, she carried much weight. Her husband respected her, asked her advice, and sometimes took it. Joseph wanted such a wife, and he hoped that Miriam would be able to develop depth in the company of his mother.

He loved her gentle, sincere nature and her unquestioning devotion to the commandments and to himself. She flattered him with her attention and single-minded efforts to prepare for marriage. But some part of him felt unready for this particular woman. He knew that they must wait a little longer. His thoughts nearly shut out the stir among the servants, but when his mother and Miriam rushed into the courtyard calling for him and his father and uncle, he ran to investigate. Perhaps a stone block had broken off the wall or someone was injured.

He reached his mother, who, when she saw him, began to sob. "Oh, Joseph, he has killed them all! Gessius is murdering our people in the upper market!"

"Mother! What? All?"

38

"Hundreds, Joseph." A young man, Joseph's age, breathless from his run from the northern part of the city, gasped out the account of the attack of the Roman soldiers on the people doing business in the marketplace. Nearly thirty-six hundred people would die that day under the Roman sword—a loss far greater than the loss of the money contained in the Temple treasury.

"I see," Joseph said slowly, stunned at the news. "Gessius has indeed flown his colors." He hurried the women into the house and stationed servants to watch. He wondered what to do next, but he could think of nothing except to wish for his father's return and to wonder if his father or uncle had been among the victims. He felt strangely compelled to pray.

4

At last Joseph saw his father and his uncle David hurrying through the outer court toward the house. Joseph breathed deeply, shivering as he dismissed the thought of their deaths.

"Mother! Miriam! They've come."

The joy of the reunion was dulled by the account the two men gave of the upper-market massacre. Friends and relatives young and old had perished in the indiscriminate murders in the streets.

"We must join the protesters. There can be no justification for such action," Matthias declared. Against the weeping protests of his wife he and the other men of the household left the villa to make their way toward the Antonia Fortress, where Florus was staying.

Soon they were in a crowd of thousands of shouting, sobbing people in Jerusalem's northern second-quarter district, outside the western gate of the Antonia Fortress. Gessius had left the Herodian Palace to set up a tribunal there. Already called "The Murderer of Jerusalem," he prepared to meet his subjects in an official capacity.

Ben Asher stood crying and chanting, his clothing conspicuously torn. Locked in the crowd, he prayed the prayer of Asaph against his enemies. "Hold not thy peace, and be not still, O God. . . . They have said, Come, and let us cut them off from being a nation; that the name of Israel may be no more in remembrance." The moans and wails of the people reached his ears, and he intensified his prayer. "O my God, make them like a wheel; as the stubble before the wind. Let them be confounded and troubled for ever;

yea, let them be put to shame, and perish: that men may know that thou, whose name alone is JEHOVAH, art the most high over all the earth."*

Inch by inch, the crowd pushed Uncle David, his nephew, and his brother-in-law toward the Gabbatha, the broad ramp where judgment was taking place. But Gessius was not calling for hearings, not making decisions in favor of or against his soldiers. He was continuing to pronounce sentences on the Jews.

From their position at a distance, Joseph, his father, and his uncle saw Gessius gesturing and knew that he was speaking. They had no indication of his words, though, until suddenly a report spread through the crowd like lightning. Matthias and Joseph were stunned anew and Uncle David staggered visibly at the pronouncement.

Gessius had ordered fifteen men of the Equestrian Order, a military band of Roman cavalry made up of native Jews, to be crucified. These fifteen had balked at Gessius' command to attack the Jews in the upper market. Now they were to pay for their refusal to kill their own kindred by pitiless and humiliating deaths on crosses.

"But it's impossible," Joseph declared vehemently. "Those men are Roman citizens as well as Jews. According to Roman law no one, not even the procurator, is allowed to execute them without a full Roman military trial before a special tribunal. That's *Roman* law. He can't do that."

But the men were marched away before their eyes. Joseph's father left his son and his brother to join the high priest's faction and try to plan some action. Joseph and ben Asher edged northwest amid the crowd toward the ancient Fish Gate. Once past that gate, which ran through the city's second northern wall, they stared at the frightening hill before them. Upon it was the well-known face of the skull, which through the centuries had been deeply

*Psalm 83:1, 4, 13, 17-18.

etched by erosion into the southern facet of gray rock.

It was called by the Hebrews *Golgotha* (skull), and by the Latin-speaking Roman troops it was called *Calvary*. It was named not only for its appearance, but also because it was the place of death—outside the city, in token deference to Jewish law. As the city expanded, however, the new, outermost third north wall placed the site within the bounds of the city. Here Jesus of Nazareth had died thirty-six years earlier, along with two other Jews, and here the fifteen men sentenced by another Roman procurator would die today.

Joseph hated the place. Everything about it spoke of death, hatred, and violence. *A distinctly Roman death,* he thought, as he watched some men building the fifteen crosses. *Painful, slow, public, removed from the judge.* People thought twice before stoning someone. To throw a stone at someone you knew, to take part in that person's death, was difficult. But this democratic dying of the Roman people was so easily begun.

Still, it did make the desired impression on the people who watched. And for some strange reason, people did watch. The fifteen men were stripped, pushed down upon the crosses, and held on the wood so that their hands and feet could be nailed. The *clunk, clunk* of the hammers, the screams of the man as the nails pierced flesh, then bone and wood, fell on a crowd oddly silent for its size. They were sounds that could not be forgotten. By now some of the wives of the Equestrians had managed to get to the front, and their cries touched Joseph deeply. He thought of his own fears earlier that day when he had thought, for the first time in his life, of the very real possibility of his father's death. *The pain involved in love and commitment is a large price, he thought,* and Miriam quickly came to his mind as he saw the women pushing toward their husbands, begging the soldiers for mercy before they were pushed away.

The soldiers in charge looked haggard and ashamed, knowing that they were crucifying fellow soldiers who had the courage to disobey an order because of their moral convictions. Yet the soldiers in charge also knew that swift penalty would be theirs if they too were to balk at this assignment. Many fought private battles that day over right and wrong, and some took hope at the thought that this illegal act might bring about the recall of His Eminence Gessius Florus to Rome for trial and, they hoped, for death.

Uncle David noted the profuse bleeding from one of the victims. "See," he told Joseph. "The nail has pierced his wrist instead of his hand. See how the blood flows. God has had mercy on him. He will be dead shortly. He will not suffer the agony of the cross's exposure for hours ahead."

Secretly, Joseph doubted the mercy of God toward that individual, but he said nothing. To Uncle David, everything seemed so clear. Why were things so difficult for him?

Joseph turned away, and his uncle followed him. Some of the victims were Joseph's own age, and as he moved out of the crowd, he stopped to breathe deeply, his back to the hill, and let the nausea pass. He tried to remind himself that Gessius was not all of Rome, that the system itself could be of benefit to him. But his views were severely challenged by the fifteen shadows that fell across the hill.

"Your father will choose moderation, wait and see," Uncle David said smugly.

"And you, Uncle? Would you prefer war?"

"I prefer that Messiah should come and rid us of this curse. 'Rejoice greatly,' " he shouted, " 'O daughter of Zion; shout, O daughter of Jerusalem: behold, thy King cometh unto thee: he is just, and having salvation.'† We pray for the fulfillment of Zechariah's prophecy, Joseph. We are still God's chosen ones, are we not?"

"Yes, Uncle David."

†Zechariah 9:9.

43

"You speak without conviction, Joseph. Do you go the way of your father, and choose politics as the answer to our dilemma?"

"I don't know, Uncle David. It's been so long since there was a prophet, unless you consider John ben Zacharias, or Jesus of Nazareth."

Uncle David snorted in contempt. "Prophets! John was a false prophet."

"You seem quite sure. Was there not a great deal of debate?"

"Never in my mind. He spoke of the Kingdom of God being at hand. It did not come, and still has not come. Therefore, he spoke lies. He was not from God. He did no miracles, and he died a wretched death."

"And Jesus? He did miracles."

Uncle David hesitated, and the pause was not missed by his nephew. "You do have some doubts about Jesus of Nazareth?"

Uncle David shrugged. "Not I. But others still think of him as some kind of spiritual leader. Messiah, no, he was not Messiah. If he had been, we would certainly not be here today, having just witnessed a Roman execution in our very own city."

Matthias had arrived home before them with news of the city leaders' decision. "We shall appeal to King Herod Agrippa," he told his family. "We are sending a delegation to speak with him. Something must be done. The Zealots will not be restrained much longer."

Four days later, Matthias and a delegation of his fellow Moderates stood before the red-bearded great-grandson of Herod the Great. He had been raised in Rome, and he had some influence there. He was also the king of Galilee and its environs. The Jews felt that he might be touched with their reasoning, that he might use his influence on their behalf. In Jamnia, near Joppa, they met him to ask advice.

This king knew that he was king only by the tolerance of Rome. He had a semblance of power, to be sure, and Rome supported him luxuriously, but in the end, Rome was the conqueror. *Why,* he wondered as he met the troubled delegation, *could these Jews not simply accept the rule of Rome? No one could govern the Jews.*

"Where are the men, where are the weapons you can count on?" he asked them, smiling. "Where is your fleet that is to sweep the Roman seas? Where are the funds to pay for your expeditions? Do you think you are going to war with Egyptians and Arabs? If you make a right decision you will share with me the blessings of peace, but if you are carried away by your passions you will go without me to your doom."

Matthias returned to Jerusalem, glowing, confident that Herod would support the Moderates, but Uncle David was unimpressed.

"Promises from any one of the Herods is like oil on the fingers: it is quickly gone."

"He cannot help but side with us against Gessius in this matter. People murdered in the streets! How can such a thing be tolerated in a civilization that claims to live by popular law?"

"The Zealots will certainly not tolerate it, you wait and see," warned the old uncle.

Joseph listened at a distance appropriate for a son and tried to envision Gessius ensconced in luxury at the fortress. But the sight of the young men on crosses kept coming back to him. He chided himself for being undecided about the Romans. Reason told him that he should hate them all, that he should invest his youth in ridding his home of their influence. But some inner note of caution told him to hold back, to wait. All about him his friends were already leaving their homes to go and fight with the Zealots in the hills and surrounding villages. They would soon be calling him.

For now, his decision was clear. He would stay at home and make money with his father. It was safe. More than that, it was sensible, for certainly money was the language of Rome, and he felt certain that it would be the image of Caesar in gold, not the swords of the Zealots or his uncle's prayers, that would someday save him.

5

News of the massacre and crucifixions reached Caesarea quickly, and those events were the main topic of conversation among the soldiers who regularly gathered at the home of Agamemnon, the Greek merchant. The men were guests of his daughter Alexandra, and as they talked, she listened discreetly as she directed the servants and arranged for the comfort of her friends. Her black hair, piled high on her head, and her olive skin radiated her Greek ancestry.

"I don't believe it," said one of the men. "Gessius would never deliberately disobey Roman law. It would be the end for him, and he's too comfortable in his position."

"What's the truth, then?" asked the listener. "Who changed the story?"

"Anyone might have made it up. But the fifteen Equestrians were Roman citizens. I don't understand." Conversation trailed off, and the soldier shook his head.

They're afraid, Alexandra thought. *They are all under the command of Gessius Florus, and they wonder if he will command well or if they will be forced to choose between conscience and duty.* The comforts of the lavish home eased the soldiers' minds for a time; and though they spoke of military life, they also joked and later began to laugh and sing.

Alexandra drew a large cushion into the circle of young men and women playing a game with sticks and dice, and watched quietly. Thaddeus would win, of course. He had invented the game. Besides, if he was ever beaten he would lose his temper and pout. Still, the game was enjoyable, and he always seemed to have people around him.

"Now, my love," said Thaddeus, with a direct look at

47

Alexandra, "watch me win, just as I said I would." He tossed the dice, rolling exactly the number that allowed him to collect the remaining sticks. "I win!," he shouted, to the surprise of no one.

"Very good," Alexandra said with a polite nod.

"She is not impressed," Thaddeus said in a confiidng tone to the others in the circle, who giggled at the exchange. "Perhaps I can beat another challenger?"

"Oh, no! Not me!" was heard amid the rustle of silken cushions as the watchers dispersed, shaking their heads and laughing.

"You seem to have lost your audience," Alexandra observed.

"Who, me? Exactly as I had planned it," Thaddeus said, and moved closer to Alexandra's side. "Will you give me an answer tonight?"

"Of course I will. The one I gave you last night, and the night before that. Thaddeus, you are a wonderful friend to me, but I do not wish to marry you."

The temper rose, and was checked. His military bearing was very evident as he tried to remain calm. "Why not?"

"You know the answer."

"Why?—apart from the fact that I am not a believer in your Christ?"

"Apart from that, I don't know. If you were a believer, I might think about whether I love you. Since you don't follow Him, I don't consider the issue at all."

"Think about it. One of these days, I might stop asking."

"I know. And that is your privilege. I do not want to make a wrong decision on so important a matter."

The guests were leaving, and Alexandra walked with Thaddeus to the door. He said, "The next time I see you, I am going to ask you to marry me again."

She nodded solemnly. "I hope and pray, Thaddeus, that the next time I see you, you will be a follower of Christ."

48

It was almost midnight as Alexandra watched the bubbles swirl around the water in intoxicating patterns as she lay soaking. The rectangular marble bath was in the secluded but central atrium of the villa, and all around she could hear the sounds of servants clearing away the leftover food from the evening's entertainment.

Alexandra poured a pinch more of the scarlet bath spice into the water. The atrium at once filled with the fragrance of the pungent pine oils, which softened the skin, and the exotic spices, which perfumed the hair. The flickering light of the oil lamp reflected the swirling patterns as the surface of the water turned a bright pink.

She thought about the conversations of the evening, the fear, and most of all the hatred. "The Jews," she had heard one centurion remark, "should be eliminated. They are the whole problem."

She wondered how it felt to be a Jew, whether they were all screaming radicals, if they all hated Romans and Greeks. Those she had seen in Caesarea were certainly no different from other humans, though of course they had their traditions, which they held near and dear.

Alexandra felt a rise of emotion as she thought about the Hebrew people. Only one did she know well, old Philip, called, "The Evangelist," who had told her of the Christ, the Savior who now filled her life. She was troubled at the thought that there was nothing she could do to help the Jews in these troubled times.

She fully believed the reports from Jerusalem. She knew that Gessius was capable of such action. She also knew that his actions were gradually turning the Greeks in Caesarea against the Jews. The Jews were openly scorned and hated, and riots were starting everywhere in small towns around Caesarea. She would see Philip soon and ask him what was to be done.

Suddenly her mother burst into the room. "Are you insane, daughter?," she shouted. "There is fighting between Jews and Romans in the city right now! Some of the men were no sooner out of our door than they were called into their units to fight. The Zealots have declared war against Rome! And here you sit, soaking as if you had nothing to do."

"Well, Mother, what am I to do?" She held back the stinging sarcasm that lingered in her mind, much as Thaddeus had held his temper earlier in the evening. *Honor your father and mother,* she remembered, a law of the Jews now obeyed by Christians as well.

"Do? First of all, you could spread the word that you are no longer a Christian."

Alexandra shook her head silently.

"I thought that would be your answer," Alexandra's mother said. "Then you must get out of this Roman city tonight. Immediately. Your father says that they may kill you. Everyone in the army knows that you're a Christian, and if the order comes to round you all up together, and even us with you—*Are you still washing?*"

"But Mother, I'm not a Jew. I'm a Greek."

"As far as the Romans are concerned, you might as well be a Jew. You worship a Jew and that's enough. A Christian—ahhh!" She raised her arms in a gesture of despair. "It isn't safe for you to stay here any longer. Hurry! Your life is in danger. And don't light any lamps. It may look suspicious."

Alexandria tried to remain calm, but she was visibly shaken by this command from her mother. "Mother, I don't want to leave. Where can I go?"

"Someplace where no one knows you. Someplace where Jews are not being killed. I don't know! Just—you can't stay here."

Alexandra stood and walked out of the luxurious bath. Quickly she dried her body and dressed in the plain brown

50

robes laid out on the marble bench.

Her mother frowned and shook her head sadly. "Look at you. They have bewitched you. You used to dress attractively and the centurions all wanted to marry you. Now, you have hidden everything. Who will marry you—a Jew carpenter? See, I know something about your beliefs. Does that surprise you?"

"No, Mother, but I'm glad. Perhaps when you know more, how Jesus came out of the grave, you will believe."

"Oh, do I hate those Jews! I hope that our Greek men join with the Romans and kill every last Jew in Palestine. They are right. The Jews are a plague and have to be wiped out."

"Mother, don't be foolish. That's murder, not any kind of justice."

Her mother was not listening. "Get dressed, Jew-Christian, and then get out of my house. I don't know you any more. At least put your hair up high on your head so that you'll look like a real Greek until you get to wherever you're going. When you're out of my sight you can take it down and look like a Hebrew peasant if you want to; I don't care."

For a moment Alexandra was still, stunned by her mother's remarks.

"I see," she said. "It's not my safety that concerns you, but your own."

"What of it?"

The old nature in Alexandra was ready with a scathing retort, but the new woman within her quelled the bitter words. Instead, she nodded silently and began to tie up her hair.

"You're right. It is wrong for me to endanger you and Father because of my beliefs. If I die, I will live with Jesus. But you must learn to love Him yet. I'll leave as soon as I can."

She left her mother alone and went to gather her belongings and make a few farewells before beginning her journey out of Caesarea.

Her father, Agamemnon, was a former Greek soldier who, years before, had been levied into a Roman legion and thus through a decade of service had won the coveted *civitas,* Roman citizenship. He had married the beautiful woman who was now his wife, and they had settled in Caesarea. Here Agamemnon began a second career and a new life, making and selling pottery, just as his father had done in Athens, the pottery center of the world.

Agamemnon idolized his daughter. She had clearly inherited her mother's classic Greek beauty. For the last half-dozen years, she had been acting more wild, more mean, and certainly more conceited than he could have imagined. She had become so evil tempered and such an ill-mannered, self-centered loudmouth that some months ago he found himself starting to hate her. His lovely little Grecian statuette had become an extravagant, unbridled beast whom he could no longer manage. He was ready to order her forever out of his house, especially when her friendships with the soldiers threatened to take on an immoral dimension.

Then she had changed, suddenly. Her loudness melted away, and she seemed preoccupied with thought rather than temper, except for momentary lapses for which she begged forgiveness. She assumed a gentility that he had always dreamed of for her. Her self-centeredness and lavish spending of his money ceased so completely that he had to caution her against the appearance of poverty. His competitors would think he was not doing well!

Agamemnon laughed at his wife and even scolded her when she declared, as she often did, that Alexandra was insane. "Mother, don't say that any more. I like the new Alexandra, and what is more, you like her, too. If this

Philip or this Jesus has changed her, I am almost ready to believe in them myself. Mother, a thousand beatings could not have produced such a change. It is indeed a miracle; she is right when she says that she has been born again. And it is this new person that I love once more. I have my daughter back, and she is now more beautiful than ever before. As Socrates said, she is now beautiful in virtue, and that is the highest beauty."

He wondered, on that night, just where his daughter might go. When she was finally ready to leave, she came to him.

"The Zealots are north of the city," he mused. "Greek or Christian, it will not matter to them. They may harm you. Antioch—I don't know."

"Father, please, let me go to Jerusalem. There are many Christians there. They will help me."

"Jerusalem—perhaps. They say that the road south is still open. Yes! I know a man there, a Jewish oil merchant, whose home is in the protected upper city. I will give you a letter, and he can direct you to some Christians, I am sure. We must hurry. There is not much time." He looked tenderly at his daughter and said, "Take care, Alexandra. Say that you are a Greek to the Greeks and Romans, and stay out of the Temple and the lower city where the rebel Jews live. The Romans are going to bring havoc to those places; you wait and see."

"I will be careful, Father. And God will not let anyone harm me until it is His time to receive me into heaven."

"That is no comfort to me, child. I want—" His voice broke, and he pulled her close to him. "I want you to come back to me, safe and alive."

She did not answer, and a tear slid down her face. "Goodbye, Father," she whispered. "Do think of the Lord while I am gone. He loves you so, as I do."

He kissed her forehead, and she turned and left him alone in the beautiful, empty house.

6

"Master," the servant intoned quietly, "there is a stranger at the gate. A woman."

Matthias rose, frowning, from the table where he and his son worked on the accounts for the family business.

"A woman? We are expecting no one. Why should a woman be traveling during this fighting? She is alone?" He asked all these questions as he hurried into the open courtyard with the servant. The servant nodded.

"I believe she traveled with the caravan now selling in the market."

Matthias reached the gate and called simply, "Who?"

Alexandra answered, "I, a friend from Caesarea."

"What is your name?"

"I am Alexandra, daughter of your patron Agamemnon Athanopolis, the pottery merchant."

"Ah!," cried Matthias in joyful recognition as he opened the door of the gate to allow Alexandra to enter. "Do come in quickly! You are most welcome in my home."

Matthias led the young woman through the courtyard toward the main part of the house, knowing that many eyes peered through the window corners. A woman alone! She was unveiled, and her hair, though it held no ornaments, was laced with cords and tied high on her head. Though not a Hebrew, she seemed to know the way of Jewish households, and waited at the door for the servants to bring water for her feet.

After the bowing and greetings and introductions were over and a welcoming meal of bread and olives had been eaten, Matthias spoke to Alexandra.

54

"What news have you from my friend Agamemnon?"

"He sends you this letter," replied Alexandra, taking the small parchment from the sash of her robe. "It was necessary for me to leave Caesarea when the insurrections began. I seek refuge in this city among friends."

"But you are Greek," said Sarah, who sat next to Alexandra at the foot of the table.

"I am a Christian as well," said Alexandra, and waited for the silent surprise to be concealed in the faces around her before she continued. "My parents thought it best that I leave the city. There is much confusion just now."

Christian! Greek!, thought Joseph as he watched his father reading the letter. *Who would have thought that such a thing should ever be in the Matthias household.* Across the table, on the left of his father, sat Uncle David, rigid, staring, betraying nothing of the frustration he felt. He had eaten nothing since the women were present. Guest or no, he felt she should have been served separately. *Christian, female, Greek. Where could she go?* Joseph wondered.

"Your father asks that we give you direction to other Christians in the city. I know of none, but perhaps we can find where they are staying. There is much fighting even here in Jerusalem, Alexandra. But you shall be our guest until we find your friends."

"But of course, I must stay at the inn," she answered, sincerely. "I could never expect such hospitality from you and your family. I am a stranger." A flicker of hope appeared in Uncle David's eye.

But no, Matthias would remain true to the teachings of his father. "We say here that every stranger is an invited guest," he replied, smiling. "Please stay the night, and tomorrow we shall talk of your leaving again."

Joseph watched her leaving the room with Sarah. Had she noticed that he was there, that he was the eldest son of an eldest son, handsome in his own right? Was her mind only on her journey, and did she really wish to leave and live among her unnoted Christians? Joseph was upset with himself at his own wishing to be noticed: he felt like a schoolboy who shows off with a sling, aiming at birds, hoping the little girls will see.

Alone that night, Sarah questioned her husband. "Is it wise, Matthias, to bring this woman into our home?"

"What else could we do? She is a guest. Should I have been rude and sent her off into the city where Zealot warriors will be at her throat and brigands at her side?"

"Of course not. But I know that you have more in mind than an overnight visit for the sake of her comfort, and that there is more to your motives than courtesy to a business account. You have given her the upper room," Sarah stated, and waited for husband to explain.

"I need the night to plan, to think, Sarah. These are difficult times. Tomorrow you may come while I discuss this with David and Joseph. Then I will be certain of the action that should be taken."

Before the morning meal was served, the family council convened. Uncle David eyed his sister suspiciously, and Matthias reproved him. "It is her home, ben Asher. She will not be excluded from the decisions that concern it."

Reproved, the old man settled onto the divan against the wall and listened.

"Listen, my loved ones," Matthias began. "This is how we live in war. Soon we will be forced to stop shipping our goods."

"Father," Joseph interrupted anxiously, "it is only a civil uprising. The Romans will destroy the Zealots any day now. Certainly it can't be so serious."

"God is not with the Romans," said Uncle David.

"And I do not believe He is with the Zealots, either," said Matthias. "But I do know the natures of Manahem and Eleazar. As long as there are men to die, they will con-

56

tinue to fight. It will get worse before it gets better. The roads will be closed. The Romans will come in force. Already the Zealots have begun confiscating caravans for supplies. They have no funds, so they steal.

"I do not fear the Zealots. We have money, and that will pacify them. But the Romans! Should they surprise us someday in a house-to-house search, what better protection could we have than the presence of a Greek whose father is a Roman citizen? What could remove us farther from the Zealot cause?"

"Then you mean for the Greek woman to stay here indefinitely?," asked Sarah.

"I do. She seems discreet, even wise. I am sure she will not trouble our household in any way, and in this time of uncertainty, she will be a great asset."

"But she is *Christian*," moaned Uncle David.

"All the better. The Zealots may be persuaded that she is a Jewess, and we shall be safe on all sides. Well?" he demanded.

When no one replied, he took their silence for acceptance. "She stays," he stated.

"But Father, what if she does not wish to stay?" asked Joseph.

Matthias thought for a moment. "I believe she will. Even Christians enjoy comfort. And besides, if we find no other Christians in the city, to whom can she go?" He smiled and winked, and Joseph found, to his embarrassment, that he was greatly relieved at the prospect of having the girl in his home.

Miriam, however, was uneasy. Never had she seen a woman so striking in appearance, so at ease in the city, even among men. Yet there was nothing improper about her, nothing showy or coarse. Money? Perhaps living in wealth gave one that particular air, though Sarah did not seem to have it. Miriam wondered if all Greek women were

57

like Alexandra. She now stood at the door of the upper room within hearing of Alexandra and addressed the servant who attended the guest.

"I wish an audience with the guest of Matthias ben Joseph and his household."

Alexandra immediately invited her into the room.

"You have brought little for such a journey," Miriam remarked.

"I left quickly. I hope to return home soon."

Miriam shook her head. "You will be staying for some time. Matthias will tell you, and you must not let him know that I told you. I heard it from the kitchen servants. He wishes that you remain in the house until it is safe for you to return to Caesarea."

"And does he feel that it may not be safe for a long time?"

Miriam nodded, preoccupied with the room and the personal articles that related to the occupant. Suddenly she saw a hand mirror and rushed to pick it up. Holding back, she looked shyly at Alexandra. "May I?"

Alexandra smiled and nodded, then watched as Miriam scrutinized her own face and hair.

"Do you have a glass in your home?"

"No. I have a plate of polished brass, but the likeness is poor."

"Please," Alexandra said, "take this one. I have nothing to give the house of Matthias, but when you come into the family, you shall bring the glass with you, and perhaps I shall be remembered."

"How did you know I should marry Joseph?"

"I see the coins in your headpiece. That means that you're engaged, doesn't it? And you certainly don't come here to see Uncle David."

They laughed together, and the friendship was sealed. They talked of custom, of womanhood, and of love and duty, and Miriam told Alexandra about her wedding plans.

"Soon we shall have the betrothal ceremony. As soon as Joseph sets the time."

"He should hurry. Another young man may ask for you."

Miriam shook her head. "It's a promise. We shall marry. Already I'm becoming part of the family, as you noticed. It is my job."

Shy again, she looked at Alexandra and asked, "What do Greek women do when they marry?"

Alexandra shrugged. "What all women do, I suppose. Bear children; obey the wishes of their husbands—if they are good wives, at least."

"Sarah says I must learn to grind and bake, even though there are servants here."

"She is a wise woman. It is not unheard of for a man to lose his wealth."

"Alexandra, did you see the soldiers in Caesarea? Are they murdering Jews, as Uncle David says?"

"Many of the soldiers are my friends. They do what they are told, and they protect the citizens against the attacks of the Zealots in Caesarea. But a few are wicked and use the opportunity to kill because they hate the Jews."

"Why do they hate us? I do not understand."

"The Jews are special," Alexandra said. "You were chosen by God to be the people through whom He sends redemption to the world. He has blessed you. The rest of the world is jealous. I know, for I once hated Jews myself."

"You?"

Alexandra nodded. "Everywhere I went in Caesarea there were Jews. They had a great number of laws and disapproved of everything I did. But then a man taught me about the teachings of a Jew named Jesus, the Christ. He made the Jewish Law come alive with meaning for me."

"Oh, yes, you are Christian. The servants told me." Miriam dismissed the subject with her guarded tone. "Uncle

59

David would not want me to listen to it, I know, and Joseph might not approve either."

She rose and left quickly, with only a formal good-bye.

After the news of the family's decision was announced, Alexandra sought out her new friend. "Miriam, please don't be afraid of me. I don't want to threaten you in any way. But following Jesus is a way of life for me now. Perhaps you will understand more later. I want to learn more of the ways of the Jews. For it is certainly true that my salvation is of the Jews."

"Women do not teach," Miriam said, still wary.

"May I go with you to the Temple?"

Miriam was startled, even shocked. "The Temple. You?"

Alexandra nodded. "I promise not to be conspicuous. And I will wear a veil. I will stay in the court of the Gentiles. Please." She wanted to say that she longed to be in all the places where her Lord had walked and spoken, even to see the place where He had died. But she knew it was not the right time.

"I will ask Joseph," Miriam said, and left her again.

Miriam often accompanied Joseph to the Temple to observe the evening sacrifice, walking slightly behind him and to his right. He had been only too happy to have Alexandra join them, and he felt unhappy at the distance that custom put between them. His father was certainly more liberal than other men in the city; still, to converse openly with a woman who was not even a family member was unheard of. He was curious about her beliefs, about her status in Caesarea, her opinion of the procurator, her association with the soldiers. She was from another world; yet here she was, wishing to learn about his world. He felt that Miriam had an unfair advantage, and that Alexandra would certainly benefit from direct conversation with him. But there was nothing to be done.

Never had Joseph seen so many people crowded into the great court of the Temple, the court of the Gentiles. It was the time of the evening sacrifice, and on this hot Sivan (May-June) evening, there must have been no less than twenty thousand people pushing and shoving to get closer to the place of sacrifice.

With the full moon still high in the star-filled sky, the white and gold top of the holy Temple still stood out clearly above the glistening inner walls. These walls separated the holy part of the Temple from the women's court and the great court. The two great pillars that guarded the entrance into the Temple sanctuary, Jachin and Boaz, rose staunchly above the heads of the milling crowds, and upon them their two bronze vine-and-pomegranate-sculptured chapiters caught the moonlight and reflected their holy glory to the onlooking throngs in every direction.

A hush ran through the crowd as a pillar of smoke suddenly lifted into the sky from the direction of the priests' court.

"Look! The smoke, the smoke!" The words were everywhere, spoken in thanks by those who saw it often and in awe and love by those pilgrims and strangers in the city who had come on long journeys to see it for the first time. The evening sacrifice had been offered upon the great altar, and the blood of the animal had been poured out before the Lord.

Alexandra was caught up in the sounds of thousands of the faithful chanting aloud repetitions of the ancient Hebrew prayers. The Aramaic dialect was heard, as was the rabbinically pure Hebrew of the Chasidim; and here and there a pilgrim from the Diaspora was heard praying or wailing in Greek or Latin.

Alexandra stood silently, her eyes toward heaven, watching the smoke ascend out of sight.

"Do you know what it means?" asked Miriam.

Joseph turned his head slightly toward the woman to hear her response.

"It is the sacrifice for sin," Alexandra responded. "As your priest has offered a lamb for the sins of the nation, so we Christians believe Jesus Christ was offered for the sins of the world. He made Himself the sacrifice for the sins of the whole world."

"And do you believe that the Lord God hears you while you pray, even here, now?"

Alexandra nodded. "Like Hannah, I pray in my heart. The Spirit of God within me carries my prayers to Him as the wind carries smoke."

Miriam turned away silently. She was confused, upset. "I'm glad I'm a Jew," she stated fervently. "Look at our beautiful Temple. The moon and the torches of the priests make the white marble sparkle. God gave us the Law, and the Temple."

"And the Messiah," Alexandra murmured. Then she added, more clearly, "I am grateful to you for bringing me."

She speaks of it as past, Joseph thought. How often he had heard the women speak of their unborn babies, hoping, praying, that they might be the mother of the Promised One. Joseph wondered at the teaching Alexandra had obviously received. *Who told her that the Messiah would be a martyr? I know of no such teaching. Surely Uncle David would never believe it.*

As for himself, he wondered if being a Jew were such a privileged thing. He thought of the crucifixion hill leering at them across the city, of all the death that haunted the walls of Jerusalem. Uncle David had never known peace, and his father's father had not known peace. All the prophets foretold the destruction of the city. Even in the day of King David the city was blighted with civil strife.

And the sacrifices! He was tired of killing, sick of blood.

62

What did it mean, anyway? Day after day after day, the Jews pleaded with God for redemption; then the Romans came and killed whomever they wished. It was an ancient system, delivered by God, but for what purpose? The sacrifice had been offered this evening, but he knew that tomorrow his sins would still cling to him.

There seemed to be no meaning, and Joseph was suddenly irritated with Miriam's shallow acceptance of their position. He looked down at her as she gazed at the Temple. Her rapt expression was childlike. But in Alexandra he saw the seriousness of one who has made a difficult decision and suffered for it, yet continued because the decision was right. Certainly Miriam would never leave her family as Alexandra had done. Her beliefs were platitudes handed down by her widowed mother and his Uncle David. And he wondered about his own beliefs—

None of the three envisioned the changes that would come to that very Temple in a few short days.

7

The Antonia fortress was at last broken into by Manahem and his men. One hundred of the original four hundred Romans still held out there. But even in such a bastion the hundred simply were not enough to hold back the many thousands of Zealots bent on avenging the blood of their kin whose burials were still fresh in their minds. The Romans were killed immediately as the invading hordes poured into the square fortress through its now open gates and over its long walls.

Later that week Manahem entered the city with the blasts of rams' horns and rode pompously through the upper city as if he were king. It was plain that Manahem, the victor of Masada, laid claim to the sole right to rule Jerusalem— and perhaps all Israel.

"What do you think of it?" said Uncle David to his brother-in-law. "Is he a king? Is he the Promised One who will deliver us from Rome?"

"He comes riding through the streets as a king," replied Matthias, "but he is certainly not meek and lowly, as the prophets suggested. Time will tell."

"Time!" cried Uncle David. "I do not have as much time as some of you. I have seen many men come and go through this city with their false claims. I *must* see Messiah before I die. The time is right!"

"Be calm, David. The Lord cannot be hurried. We lived in Egypt for four hundred years before He sent Moses to deliver us. Time does not mean to Him what it means to us. To Him a thousand years are as a day."

Uncle David would not be comforted. He paced the

room, unable to concentrate on his work. Matthias quietly tallied up his orders and made small notes about the destinations and arrivals of oil shipments, waiting for his emotional brother-in-law to settle himself.

"You see, Matthias, I am afraid." He turned to the younger man. "There have been so many men with so many motives. Could I—is it possible that Messiah has already come and I did not know Him?"

Matthias turned and frowned. "What makes you say such a thing, David? You know the Scriptures. All your life has been spent in watching. How could you ever have missed Messiah's coming? Would we not be free of Rome if He had already come?"

"Yes, of course, if—"

"Yes?"

"If I have been looking for the right thing. Frankly, Matthias, I am puzzled by the girl Alexandra."

"Ahh, I see. Joseph has been telling you of her beliefs."

David ben Asher hung his head, embarrassed. "I listened to her myself as she spoke with the servants. Matthias, she seems so sure! She loves the Jews; she rejoices in the promise that salvation is of the Jews. I have never known such a person. She knows little of the Scripture, but all the things she tells me of Jesus of Nazareth could be true of the Messiah."

"And you believe it?"

The big man threw his hands in the air. "Who can tell? And I say, Matthias, I must know. I cannot keep waiting for men to appear and claim to be Messiah, and then wait and see if they really are. I must know Him when He comes, or know if He has come already."

"And how will you learn?"

"I know of no other way than to search the Scriptures. And I shall do that more diligently than ever. Matthias, don't you care? Does Messiah mean nothing to you?"

Matthias nodded solemnly. "I know that with Messiah will come a new life. What it will be, I do not know. But I trust the Lord. I do not believe He will allow one so sincere as you to miss the coming of Messiah. And I believe that when He comes, you will know."

Matthias rose from his work and said, "Come, brother. We will go to the Temple, where you may hear the rabbi. It will strengthen your heart. I must go to the olive yards and speak with the workers there."

"Is the city safe?"

"I understand that Manahem seeks only Romans, and that with a vengeance. The Temple should be safe at any rate."

*   *   *

The press of the crowd prevented the trio of men from the Matthias household from gaining entrance into the treasury court, also known as the court of the women. The emotions evident among the crowd were frightening, as the hostile people shouted, "Death to Manahem, murderer of the high priest!" Raucus catcalls came from every direction as people showed their complete disdain for the self-appointed monarch whom they had so recently acclaimed.

"What is this!" cried Uncle David. "Someone has killed a priest?"

"Manahem," answered a friend nearby. "He was rooting out Roman sympathizers and murdered—yes, I say it!— brutally murdered Ananias."

Matthias was aghast. "Ananias was not a Roman sympathizer. He was a Moderate, a leader."

"Reason enough for Manahem."

The thoughtful silence of the two men seemed to spread over the crowd as the evening sacrifice began.

Though too far away to observe the proceedings, Joseph knew that the evening offering, welcoming the Sabbath, was being offered.

Suddenly there was a shriek, and excited shouting could be heard from the court. "Manahem," came the word. He stood in the treasury court himself to welcome the Sabbath. Whispers describing his regal garments passed from man to man. He had apparently determined to face the crowd—boldly, but surrounded by the daggers of his Sicarii allies, the professional killers among the Zealots. Many people lowered their eyes and heads in terrified submission. It seemed that Manahem indeed was to be the ruler of Jerusalem, with or without the consent of the people.

David ben Asher, his face contorted with anger and shame, shouted, "Is all Jewry afraid of this second King Saul who slays the priests of God?"

Matthias patted his arm. "Quiet, brother. It will not help."

Then they heard strange sounds from the holy priests' court within. Then they heard shouts and screams and the sound of rocks striking the sacred stone walls. "What is happening?" Uncle David demanded. He stood on tiptoe to see over the heads of the crowd, all of whom were on tiptoe themselves. He began to bully his way through the crowd, and since they could not stop him, Matthias followed.

Surging into the treasury court, ringed by protesting observers whom Uncle David pushed aside, they saw Eleazar's men stoning Manahem.

"He's trapped!" shouted Uncle David. "They have him by the altar and will stone him to death."

"No!" cried Matthias, for at that moment Manahem escaped through a nearby door into a side chamber.

Throughout the night, Manahem's Zealot followers quietly disappeared. The following morning, Eleazar's tireless hounds found Manahem himself hiding in the Ophel, the northernmost height of the oldest portion of the section known as David's City. His once-grand garments were now

67

shamefully soiled. His debasement and capture were, to the delight of everyone's sense of justice, almost identical in misery to his own apprehension of the high priest not forty-eight hours earlier.

It was a public display that morning, in utter disregard for the Sabbath. And a display it was, rivaling the most gruesome Roman gladiatorial scenes. Joseph remembered those circuses, and his feelings then had been the same as his feelings at this moment.

Mercy, he begged Eleazar inwardly. *Show mercy if you would lead us, if you are the one sent from Jehovah.*

But under the stares of multiplied hundreds, the spotlessly white-clad priest personally supervised the torturing of Manahem and Absalom, the chief accomplice. A look of utter despair and agony was upon Manahem's face as they held him down to allow the sledgehammers to break his arms and legs. Joseph turned and began to push through the crowd, disgusted, disappointed. Eleazar, though he might be judicially right, was certainly no better than his opponent. Something out of the ordinary caught his attention as he made his way through the narrow, crowded streets. He stopped, turned suddenly, and saw Alexandra hiding in a doorway. Fear encircled him immediately, and he molded it into anger as he stormed toward her with a scowl on his face.

"So you choose to bring dishonor to the house of Matthias, do you. Come out of there—huddled in a doorway like a street woman!"

"I'm sorry. I only came to see what was happening."

"It is not for women to see. Look at you! Anyone for a mile could tell you are a Greek. Do you think the Zealots would spare you?" *She is beautiful,* Joseph thought, suddenly overcome with her presence. "Tell me, in Caesarea did your father allow you to walk alone in the streets?"

"When it was safe," she retorted, "before the Jews made

68

all the trouble." He reached to strike her. He was immediately ashamed, though, and his hand fell limp.

"I'm sorry," they said together, then smiled at each other.

"Joseph, I meant no harm. I followed you. I had no idea it would be so grim and ugly. I thought there might be a crucifixion, and though I dreaded it, I wished only to see the way my Lord suffered. And—oh, please forgive me for what I said about the Jews. I didn't mean it."

"Then why did you say it?"

"It is the way I am. I must always be disciplining my tongue, and sometimes I fail."

"You would make a good Jew," he said, the anger completely gone. "My mother showers words like hail sometimes. It is a gift common among women. Come, I'll take you home."

She followed him as he led the way. He tried not to look back, not to be anxious over her, not to ask if he were walking too fast, not to ask if her sandals rubbed on her feet as she stumbled along the rough street. *Why should I care?* he thought. But the very fact that she had left a secure house—probably sneaked out—to learn something new, even to share in suffering, thrilled him in a strange way.

"You know my mother will scold you unmercifully," he said.

She nodded, her face grim. "It cannot be helped. I've done what I have done. Joseph—" she looked up, alarmed, "have I really dishonored your house? Do your friends think I am bold?"

He shrugged. "You are Greek, obviously. Many Jews think all Greeks are barbarians."

"And you? Do you think so?"

"I think very little, except about olive crops and oil markets. I am too busy to philosophize. I'll be quite rich, you know. My father is very wealthy, and of course I am the firstborn son, so—"

69

"Are we almost home? I'm getting very tired."

Insulted, he quickened his pace. "Yes," he stated abruptly. *Maddening woman,* he thought. *How can she care so little about important things and care so much about the fringe areas of religion?*

Later, Uncle David told him that Manahem had finally been killed with a sword.

"So that is the fate of the would-be king of Israel," Joseph said.

"You didn't have to wait long to learn whether this one was the true Messiah, brother," said Matthias.

"No, and I know it cannot be Eleazar. He is no savior. He is an executioner without regard for the Law."

Matthias sighed. "Perhaps we will not have to worry about the Romans coming to destroy us. We can do it ourselves."

8

Gessius Florus had retreated to Caesarea. A month after the upper-market massacre he still brooded and rehearsed the incident, looking out into the darkness, seeking a solution.

"Light another torch," he ordered the elderly prefect, Epaenetus. "And bring a flagon of wine and some chicken."

The *click-clack* of a woman's sandals striking the marble floor could now be heard coming forward from the rear of the bleak, white-walled hall.

"Is it you, Octavia, my pet?"

"Yes, Gessius, it is I. I've brought you some food, wheat bread, cheese, and a knuckle of pork with red Italian wine."

The white walls of the hall reflected the flames from the torches and silhouetted the shapeliness of the Mediterranean beauty clad in a filmy green robe. She carried the tray with both hands and smiled assuringly at her husband. She stepped in front of the flustered Epaenetus and said aloud, "Epaenetus, you needn't fetch my husband food; I have brought it."

The old prefect turned silently to the procurator, who nodded his approval to his wife's orders. The prefect said, with a bow of his head, "Very good, my Lady Octavia."

As the aged prefect continued his plodding exodus to the rear with almost silent steps, he contrasted sharply with the noisy clacking of Octavia's lively walk. Her slim body seemed to flow along the aisle like a brook rippling over rocks.

"Did you hear?" mourned Gessius to his approaching wife. "This morning the Jews of Jerusalem refused to offer upon their altar the sacrifice we give to them each day in the name of the emperor. And what is worse, some fool named Manahem led a Zealot force down to the fortress of Masada and took it from our soldiers by surprise! They posed as traders, and once they got in they slaughtered everyone. Oh, how these Jews never let up in their torment of every Roman whose unhappy lot it has been to be assigned the procuratorship of Judea."

"Here, Gessius, taste a morsel of this pork. It is a double delicacy here in Palestine."

"Ah, Octavia, without your comforting presence I would this day end it all with one swift thrust of a sword."

"Gessius, don't talk foolishly. The greatest Roman generals have had to put down rebellions. Even Gaius Julius Caesar."

With his mouth stuffed with pork, he interrupted. "Ah, my pet, you don't understand. Generals who *put down* rebellions may indeed become famous, but Nero and Cestius Gallus, the governor of Syria, will accuse me of *starting* this revolution. They will claim that I started it by ordering our soldiers to attack the Jerusalem upper market last month. Nero and Gallus will hate me for it—just as the Jews hate me for it."

"Nonsense. The Jews of Jerusalem had to be taught a lesson! And all the Jews of Palestine still have to be taught this lesson. Look what Nero himself did to the Christians in Rome. We live in a new world today, and Rome rules Palestine, not the Jews. For their own good, they must accept that. They will never learn by talk. Like a rebellious child, they must be beaten into submission."

At this she stuffed a cube of cheese into his heavy lips and reaffirmed, "They had to learn a lesson in Jerusalem, and your soldiers taught it to them. If they still have to learn, then you can teach them some more."

"Yes, but I am sorry that I got excited and ordered the killing."

"Oh, Gessius, they brought that on themselves. Don't waste your sympathy on people who publicly insult Rome and her authority. What did they expect when they pelted you like a dog? Gessius, it is not your fault!"

"My procurator," the voice of the prefect was heard calling from the rear.

"Yes, yes, what is it? More bad news?"

"Yes, my procurator. It is said that fighting is breaking out in many of the towns. The Zealots have taken Macherus, but in Ptolemais the soldiers and people have driven out every Jew from the city. It seems as though a full-scale rebellion is on—in the whole country, not just in Jerusalem. Shall we send to Governor Gallus in Antioch of Syria for help?"

Gessius shook his head and sighed again.

"Is there no end to my torments? If I send for Gallus, he will curse me as incompetent while he marches his legion from Antioch all the way to Jerusalem. If I do not send for his help, these radical Jewish Zealots may take the whole country. If the rebellion succeeds, Governor Gallus will blame me; if he comes and quells it, he will get all the glory. And what of my career?" He was angry, ashamed, and incompetent before his wife. "It is all the fault of those stupid bureaucrats in Rome for not giving me a legion with which to protect myself and my authority! All the troubles in Judea through the years have come because they keep our Roman legion way up north two hundred fifty miles away where they simply grow fat and do no one any good. Without a legion kept in Judea, they tempt the Jews to revolt."

The sight of Octavia's embarrassment for him as her previous sympathy turned to contempt made Gessius decide to act quickly.

73

"Epaenetus, send a messenger to His Excellency Cestius Gallus, Governor of Syria and Commander of the Twelfth Legion, to the effect that religiously inspired fanatical Zealots, led by one Manahem, have revolted against Roman rule, have refused Caesar's sacrifice in Jerusalem, and are attempting rebellion.

"Ask him to—no, tell him that I *demand* troops be sent at once to quell these radicals."

"Good," Octavia said, smiling again. "It is done, and soon the rebels will feel the mighty heel of Rome."

"Ah, my beautiful one, if it were only so simple. I will be fortunate not to feel the heel myself before this unhappy trouble is done. Don't look so surprised," he said, laughing at her stricken face. "I know you've considered the possibility, perhaps made plans. If I am recalled, to whom will you go?"

Without waiting for an answer, he kissed her and, leaving her alone in the great hall, walked down the marbled aisle and out into the wind-chilled Caesarean night. His prefect ran behind to keep up with him.

"Centurion, centurion," Gessius called into the blackness. Meanwhile he rushed about to do what he could to limit the success of the rebels until the reinforcements would arrive. He well knew that Cestius Gallus was no friend of his and might wait weeks, allowing the situation to deteriorate totally before coming to a triumphant rescue. Gessius knew that he had to continually send the right messages north and even west so that everyone would know that he was doing his utmost and that it was Gallus' duty to come at once.

My first priority, Gessius thought to himself as his centurion lieutenants began to arrive, *is to keep Caesarea from falling to any surprise Zealot attack and keep myself alive and my private funds safe.*

"Send word, centurion," Gessius ordered, pointing, "to

every outpost in this city that they are to make immediate preparations against any surprise Jewish attack against this city."

Then, turning to another centurion, he ordered, "See that our garrison inside the city takes every precaution against a Jewish uprising from within. The Jews have short memories. They will have forgotten by now how they were crushed a few weeks ago after that Temple incident, and they may try again. Gather up every adult male Jew, especially the troublemakers, and see that you allow no rebellion to erupt upon us from within. Understand?"

"Yes, my procurator." With a smart salute of the straight right hand and forearm snapped across his breastplate, the centurion turned away. A large hand upon his shoulder halted him.

"I ask you, centurion, do you understand my intent, as well as my words?"

The confused soldier stammered a moment until Gessius Florus reached out and touched the gleaming sword at the officer's side.

"Jews are notoriously unreasonable. The fewer, the better."

*   *   *

"Well, lieutenant? Are we ready to rescue that bungler Gessius?"

"General Messala declares that the gates are open and that our army is ready to leave Antioch, General Gallus," came the stiff reply.

It was still early morning. Mounted on his mammoth black stallion, the aged, white-bearded general was the picture of the dignity and imperial pomp of the Roman Empire. His uniform—breastplate, red-plumed helmet, and scarlet cape blowing in the wind—was a sight to stir any Roman's heart. Cestius Gallus, general of the army and Roman governor of Syria, was now personally commanding the Twelfth Legion, the Fulminata—"The Thundering Ones." He looked both confident and excited. He smiled as he contemplated this opportunity to command soldiers on an expedition once again. Though Gallus often complained, everyone saw that he was obviously proud to be a leader.

"Good," replied Gallus in a soft voice mellowed with years, "at last we are ready. We shall cross the River Styx to the gloomy underworld of Jerusalem and rescue its incompetent procurator. If it were not for the insult those mad Jews of Jerusalem have given to Rome, I would be the first to leave Gessius to the torments of the frenzied rebels. Ha!" The very thought made the general laugh.

"Lieutenant Quintius, sound the first trumpet for the cavalry to begin the march."

Over the music of the trumpet could be heard the thumping of thousands of hooves on the cobblestone road that led south out of Antioch, a city named for the third-century Greek kings of Syria. Soon a second trumpet sounded and the innumerable cohorts and maniples of infantry also began the journey. The auxiliaries, laden with baggage and huge siege engines, joined the procession. Finally the last trumpet sounded and the rear guard closed the line of marching Romans.

* * *

Some weeks later the huge Roman army out of Syria encamped five miles north of Caesarea, having made its way around Mount Carmel and the Armageddon Gap between the mountains. Inside the general's dark scarlet tent, ranking Roman officers from both the Twelfth Legion and the indigenous garrison of troops of Gessius Florus were taking part in a war council. General Cestius Gallus paced up and down his long tent, waving his hands in vivid gestures of emotion. Two dozen Roman soldiers with spears held vertically were posted around the tent as guards.

76

"Why wasn't I told the full story when your procurator sent for me and my legion?" demanded Gallus, looking menacingly at the pale Marcus Cotta, a classic dark-haired Italian centurion representing Gessius at the meeting.

Gallus continued with a voice of feigned incredulity. "Amazing! Your procurator's letters gave me the impression that one city, Jerusalem, had rebelled against Rome and that I was to bring my troops and siege equipment here to take back the city! He deliberately kept from me the fact that the entire nation had rebelled in a death struggle and that no single legion would be sufficient to put it down!"

The centurion replied, "But General Gallus, Jerusalem is the key. And undoubtedly the procurator did not know when he wrote to you that all Judea would rebel."

"Do you, Marcus Cotta, lie to me?"

"No, my general, but—"

"But of course you lie, because you represent Gessius, who has given you no more information than he gave me. He was wise not to come in person. I would personally punch his fat belly. Let me tell you the facts, Marcus. When Gessius Florus sent for my legion he already knew that the rebellion was widespread. It started at his own instigation in Caesarea. Though I distrust the man, he is still a half-alert procurator. He knows the activities of his subjects. Now here I am with only one legion of six thousand. The other twenty-four thousand auxiliaries are really little more than schoolboys."

Lieutenant Quintius frowned. "But general, you told me that we had thirty thousand trained troops and that there was no cause for fear."

"I didn't know at that time that we would be fighting an entire nation of Jews who had lost mothers and brothers to Rome. They will be fighting with a zeal and hatred no single legion can possibly subdue. Yes," he said sarcastically, turning again to Marcus Cotta, "I heard about the upper-market slaughter. Believe me, Gessius has given them a grudge against Rome that will not be buried until every Jew in Palestine or every Roman in Palestine dies. The situation Gessius has put us in offers us no choice. We must now slaughter the Jews before they slaughter us."

An old soldier, a tribune, spoke. "Then what shall we do, Gallus? Shall we take our Twelfth Legion back to Antioch until we can get legions from Alexandria and Rome to reinforce us?"

"Oh, if only it were as easy as all that. If we retreat without even reaching Jerusalem, we'll dishonor our legion, dishonor Rome, and encourage these Jews to greater rebellion, if that is possible. Already the Zealots have taken—look here at the map—Jerusalem, the Herodian fortress of Masada, and Macherus."

Gallus accepted a goblet of wine and continued his evaluation. "What I really fear is staying too long in Jerusalem— for indeed we must begin there—and allowing a hundred thousand Zealots first to cut off our supply lines from Antioch and then to trap us deep in southern Israel.

"We must hit them hard and hit them fast, and then leave promptly." Gallus paused and then pointed at his younger fellow general, Messala, and continued to plan. "You, Messala, will take part of our troops and attack the seaport of Joppa, while I march the main force to strike against Jerusalem. Before you join me, you must so terrorize them in Joppa that the Zealots will get the impression that we have two legions. That way, they will think that any attempt to surround us will be futile."

As he concentrated on strategy, Gallus relaxed and for a time forgot his feelings toward Gessius Florus. And as Gallus gathered his men about him to plan, the centurion from Caesarea quietly left the tent unnoticed, glad to be gone, and even now glad that he would not be included in the vast maneuvers being planned in the general's tent.

Nine days later, on the twenty-ninth of Tishri (September-October) the unwieldly snake of thirty thousand Romans out of Syria approached the Beth-horon mountain passes, which provided the gateway to Jerusalem from the northwest. The hot summer had almost been spent. The troops, carrying about sixty pounds per man, plodded along, waiting for the west-to-east noonday sea breeze to cool them off.

After two hours Gallus, astride his large black steed, had traversed the pass, but not without great apprehension, for the mass of his troops were still behind him. To the north rose the 3,300-foot summit of the Judean peak of Ball Hazor. To Gallus' immediate south rose Mount Haruah, 2,530 feet in elevation. The soldiers marched between these peaks, stretched out in a thin, vulnerable line that vanished amid the twists and turns of the valley pass.

Then, at the moment of high noon, Quintius raced up to his commander with alarming news. "My general, the quaestor sends word to you of an ambush."

"Where, when?"

"The Zealots have fallen upon our rear baggage trains. They raced down from the sides of the valley and started to shoot and slaughter our men who were laden with the baggage wagons."

"What of our rear guard? Did they not come forward to rescue them?" asked Gallus in desperation.

"My general, the battle only lasted for a few minutes. The Jewish Zealots attacked only our unarmed baggage transporters. When the rear guard arrived, the Zealots had already fled. They would not do battle as men with our soldiers."

"Did they seize much baggage?"

"No, my general. But there was much loss of life."

"How many men died?"

"The quaestor says that almost five hundred men were slaughtered—but most of them were slaves; few Romans perished."

"Curse that rear guard. I told them to stay close."

"But general, the valley was narrow, and the attack was a surprise."

"Leave me—and, yes, at least order the rear guard closer now. Those Jews will pay in blood for this treachery."

* * *

Two days later the first scout section of the Roman legion climbed Mount Scopus and beheld before them the wondrous walled city of Jerusalem. The white limestone and pink ashlars sparkled with the sunlight.

The soldiers were breathless, and their centurion shouted, "It is as glorious as the Athenian Acropolis, which I saw ten years ago! See that white-and-gold-trimmed building with the two pillars? You can just make them out at this angle. It is the sacred Temple of the Jews; I have heard of it. Its beauty rivals that of the Roman Forum. And look at those walls! See, there are three of them, one inside the other, and a fortress, which separates us from the Temple. Ha, I wonder if the Procurator Gessius ever told General Gallus what we were up against. No one legion is going to take this city! Ah, well, that is not for us to decide. Let's get going and send our report back to the general. He's waiting to hear our news, and ha! do we have a description for him this time!"

* * *

For two days the Romans waited, watching. Then the attack began.

Alexandra watched as Joseph, his father, and Uncle David left for their work. Anxiously she gazed after them until Miriam interrupted her thought.

"Why are you standing here? Have you no work?"

"Oh! Yes, yes, I have work. I'm sorry. I was—" She had intended to say, "I was praying," but had hesitated.

"I know. I saw you. There are better things for young women to do than to look after men, especially when they will marry another."

"I am concerned for their safety. The fighting worries me."

"It has nothing to do with us. The Zealots and Romans are at war. We are not."

Alexandra bristled. "Don't you understand? Things change moment by moment in wars. The Romans are skillful. They are in the north now, but they could appear in the south at any time. The men might not be able to reenter. They should bring their stores in soon."

"And you should not say what men should do. Joseph and his father know what must be done."

"It's a good thing," Alexandra retorted, "because you women seem never to think of anything."

Miriam said nothing, but Alexandra saw the tears that sprang to her eyes. Miriam left the room quietly.

"Miriam, I'm sorry." But the words went unheard—or unheeded. Alexandra followed Miriam to apologize.

Miriam stood in the courtyard, waiting for her future mother-in-law to accompany her to the market. She did not look at Alexandra as she approached.

Her arms open, Alexandra spoke to the girl. "Please, Miriam, forgive me. I was so unkind."

"But honest."

"No, not really. I have many things to learn. Among the Jews, much is different. I have learned to care for the affairs of the city. You care for your home. I must learn your way."

At last Miriam looked at her. "We have a saying, 'Whoso keepeth his mouth and his tongue keepeth his soul from trouble.' "

Alexandra accepted the reproach silently. Suddenly Miriam snapped, "It will do no good for you to learn our ways. You are not a Jew, and Joseph will never love you."

"Love me?"

Miriam nodded. "You want him, I know. Can you deny it? No, it is true. Well, Joseph will not be charmed and neither will I." Again she deserted the other woman.

Alexandra stood, confused and wondering. *I care nothing for Joseph,* she thought. *But could it be that Miriam feels that he cares for me? He doesn't care for me.*

Alexandra hurried to make ready for the trip to market, dreading it, but anticipating the chance to find and speak to some Christian women. She felt so alone.

And, oddly, Joseph came to her mind as she considered her loneliness. He would be easy to love, if such an option were available. She found that she thought of him as they did the marketing, buying things he liked, going places he went, hearing people speak his name to Sarah. She glanced guiltily at Miriam, who was intent, as usual, on the job at hand.

Foolish woman, she chided herself. *How could I even think of Joseph? He isn't a Christian, and more importantly, he is to marry Miriam.* Alexandra prayed silently for more love for Miriam, and for none at all for Joseph.

9

For five days the attack on the north wall went forward in the standard Roman opening procedure against a walled city. There were no apparent results. Roman siege engines smashed great rocks against the walls and over them while archers shot arrows by the thousands in vain at Hebrew shadows guarding the high wall.

It was then decided that the section of the north wall which lay immediately in front of the Temple plateau would be a better place to attack. This portion was built with gigantic limestone ashlars, and it was less than an eighth of a mile in length. As the Romans faced this section of the wall, to their right stood the Antonia, which was the castle fortress built by Herod the Great in honor of Marc Antony. Earlier it had been taken from the Roman garrison by the Zealots. Attack against this Praetorium was useless for here to the right of the Romans, their flank was exposed to any sudden Zealot attack sallying from out of the fortress.

As the men of the Twelfth Legion faced the Temple Wall on their left was the old eastern wall, which separated the city from the deep gorge of the Kidron Valley. The depth of the Kidron Valley made attacking the eastern wall unthinkable, and no general or tribune who had once gazed upon the valley ever even suggested it to the puzzled General Gallus. Thus with the east wall to their left flank and the supreme Antonia to their right, the Romans went to work against the selected wall area like surgeons carefully cutting flesh.

After days of fruitless hammering, Gallus called for the testudo. It was the second strategy in the list of standard procedures for Roman fighters, and good enough for him, since it was Gessius's war. Why waste imagination and effort on his behalf?

The testudo, or "the back of a tortoise," was a protective roof of shields held over the heads of soldiers staying close to one another, rank after rank, as they moved forward. The general ordered his combat commander to have the Seventh Cohort of Infantry form the testudo against the wall so that burning torches, catapults, and rams could be brought forward under cover of the raised shields.

Against this the Zealots' resistance was unparalleled. Thousands of arrows, darts, javelins, huge rocks, torches of fire, and boiling pitch were dropped from the walls onto the suffering Roman soldiers below. Gallus watched his men obey—and die by the score, and the wall remained.

The next morning General Gallus shocked both Romans and Jews by suddenly giving the order to lift the siege and prepare for the march back to Antioch.

"But general," pleaded the younger still determined Messala, "the Jews we captured fleeing the city over the walls by night say that there is pandemonium and chaos within and that the Zealots will capitulate if we sustain the attack for another few weeks!"

"Messala," responded Gallus, "with a Roman sword at their necks, what do you expect captives to say? The winter rains will soon come—then our siege engines in the mud will be worse than useless and we will be stuck here for months. And then the Zealots from all Judea and the north may surround us—that is a possibility which must be considered. Besides, our assault on the walls thus far has accomplished nothing. It will take a larger force than we have over a year to starve this city out. I cannot risk losing my entire legion on your hunches based on the testimony of frightened captives. Prepare your cohorts to move out in the morning. I will not rot here and lose twenty thousand men in the process for the sake of that worthless procurator, Gessius, who hasn't even had the courtesy to stop his drinking for a day and come to consult with us."

"But general—"

"I know you don't approve of my decision, General Messala, but I am older and I hope wiser than you, and I'm still in charge here. In a couple of years you will be commanding legions yourself, and you can then besiege cities as long as you want. I'm too old for you to change me now, so don't try. I'm not risking losing a legion just to please Gessius—or you. We can still leave with honor. Now go and ready your troops for the march home."

General Messala, with reddened face, quickly saluted and stormed out of the tent in an obvious rage. As he left, he screamed at the lieutenant, not caring if Gallus heard, "We are throwing away an easy victory because the animal of a procurator was too ignorant to pay a courtesy call on General Gallus, and because General Gallus resents saving Gessius's kingdom for him. I wonder if the gods above settle the fate of empires on the basis of courtesy calls! Ah, I cannot change the general or the gods! Bring my horse! There is work to be done." More calmly he informed the lieutenant, "We begin our 'triumphal return' at daybreak, and it will take me all night to think up some plausible explanation to tell the troops about why we're leaving now. *Vale!* Farewell."

From its camp at Mount Scopus, the dispirited Roman army began its slow exodus. Somehow the men could not get moving. The third day after the order to depart, they reached the treacherous Beth-horon passes, fifteen miles to the northwest of Jerusalem.

Gallus and Messala, both mounted on horses, were pointing together at the passes. The younger man was anxious about their position. "Gallus, these frenzied Zealots killed nearly five hundred of our men when we entered these

85

passes. At that time they feared us and despaired of their own safety. Now that they have seen us march away from their city, they are convinced that their god is with them and that they are conquerors of the world. Their attacks will know no bounds when our auxiliaries are caught with their heavy equipment at the bottom of these passages. Already there are reports that large bands of Zealots trail us to slay our stragglers. Let me kill the mules carrying the supplies we no longer need. Why should they impede us? We can resupply at Caesarea—at Gessius' expense!"

"Good, I like that! Kill the mules, Messala, and burn everything you abandon so that nothing falls into the Zealots' hands. Only the mules pulling the siege equipment must be preserved."

"Gallus, let me burn the engines. It is the only way we can get through the pass without sustaining heavy losses."

"No, Messala, no. The engines we keep."

"But general, there isn't sufficient space in some of those defiles for me to put infantry on the sides of the siege engines. They can't be protected and they'll be used against us if captured."

"Then station your infantry on the ridges."

"They are not mountain climbers! The men are carrying equipment."

Gallus flushed with rage, and his elderly voice broke as he shouted, "Messala, the Jews seem to be mountain climbers! Why not your infantry?"

"The Jews carry little," Messala shouted back. "And they certainly are not encumbered with siege engines."

"Go, Messala, and obey. That is all."

"Yes," he answered in a bitter voice, *"General* Gallus. *Vale."*

Three hours later the heavily burdened auxiliaries, now placed in the middle of the march train, suddenly heard the shouts of the Zealots from the precipices above. Huge rocks began to roll down the sides of the Beth-horon heights, clogging the passages even more. Then the rain of arrows and darts again started to fall on the Roman soldiers, many of whom were veterans of innumerable battles and victories. Within moments it once more became apparent that Roman infantrymen, trained for disciplined battles on huge plains but now hurling javelins upward, were no match for the Zealot ambushers hurling their poisoned darts downward. To make matters worse, the Zealots were spread out and hidden in the crags and foliage above, while the Romans were crowded together in the defile beneath.

Some Romans bolted from their ranks and began to rush up the slopes to pursue the Zealots on the steep hillsides. Instantly they were cut down by the darts and arrows. The heavily armed Romans with breastplate, helmet, shield, shin guards, pack, lance, and sword, were ideal slow-moving targets for the onslaught of arrows and rocks from above. Soon the Zealots were shrieking in victory at the success of the ambush.

The trapped Romans below, despairing of all hope of safety, began to scream their emotions of horror and shame. More and more of the soldiers began to cast aside their equipment so that they could escape the passes more quickly, and this abandoned equipment moments later impeded the feet of their comrades behind. All was chaos, and death lurked beside every man. It was no battle. The Romans were butchered and their cries of despair told the story completely.

"Move in the *celerites,* the swift cavalry," ordered General Messala, screaming to be heard above the battle sounds. "First maniple on the north ridges, second on the south ridge! Make way for the third maniple to get in and clear out the valley."

"General," a centurion replied, "our cavalry cannot get through into the valley. A siege engine has fallen over, and the way is blocked. The horses cannot climb over it!"

"Then we must move it. Hurry, centurion, we must relieve those being attacked!" He darted forward into the mob of his own troops ahead, two of his subordinates pushing behind him. The situation was desperate, and Messala, cursing Cestius Gallus in his heart, knew that there was little he could do.

At last the blessed darkness fell and the attack ceased. General Gallus was on the verge of emotional collapse, so staggering were the casualty reports. Some 5,300 infantrymen and auxiliaries had been slain, and another 380 cavalry had been lost on the hillsides while attempting to drive away the Zealots. The back of the Twelfth Legion had been broken by an irregular band of guerrillas avenging themselves in this one valley for years of murderings at the hand of the procurator and the Gentile Romans.

Gallus was a desperate man, and he conceived a desperate plan.

"Messala, choose one light cohort of four hunderd men to remain in camp this night with torches burning, standards high, and the siege engines and wagons all in place. The Zealots will believe that we are encamped for the night. Meanwhile, under cover of darkness we will move the main force west to the plains by an all-night forced march. That is my order! I want no discussion of it! All units move out at midnight, except for the cohort that remains."

Messala gasped. "The four hundred will die, and the enemy will take our engines and standards!"

"Curse you, Messala!" cried Gallus. "I said I didn't want any discussion. I choose to take twenty-four thousand Romans to safety. Our fulminata will return again with other legions and we will yet slit the throats of these Jewish rebels! Would you prefer that I give them another morning to see if they can slaughter another five thousand or ten or fifteen before we get out of these passes? Now get out and do your duty this time! You talk well, but earlier today you did not rescue the auxiliaries, did you? Do you think you can do better tomorrow in the passes again, with all the debris there forcing all wagons almost to a stop?"

Sobbing with rage, but not daring to contradict the general openly, Messala thundered, "If only those Zealots would fight us on a plain, I would destroy them in one hour."

"General Messala," Gallus responded, overly calm, "they don't fight on the plain. That is why they are such pestilent foes. They fight from city walls and from precipices when Romans are helpless below. That is why we need to bring four legions down upon them until we starve them into submission the way rats must be starved out of their holes. Now leave!"

Messala ran from the tent and stood beneath the Palestinian sky, crying. "If only we had stayed," he moaned, "at least they might have died in battle. And how will I choose the four hundred?" The stars gave him no answers, and no peace, and he could only go about his unwelcome task.

By two hours after dawn on the next morning the ruse was discovered by Simon ben Giora, the rough and rude Zealot attack commander. But it was too late. The Romans had by this time reached the plain of Sharon and to engage them there would bring instant vengeance and death, if not excruciating tortures, to every pursuing Zealot. Cestius Gallus had fled in utter defeat and shame, leaving behind the Twelfth Legion's siege engines, its precious standards, and its honor.

Worst of all, he left four hundred of their bravest Roman foot soldiers for a final sacrifice to the bloodthirsty Zealots. Simon lifted his arm and brought it down, the signal for ten thousand Zealots to rush down and destroy the final maniple of Roman infantry. Death reigned, and now that both Rome and Israel had enough blood that needed to be avenged, the continuation of the war was guaranteed.

*   *   *

Secure in their upper-city villa, Joseph, his family, and their guests observed the effects of the Zealot war.

"Have the Romans been beaten, Father?"

"It would seem so—this group, at least."

Joseph frowned. "I don't think so. Just because a Roman army leaves the area, it does not mean they are beaten. There are many, many Romans. I believe they will return."

"And then?"

Joseph shrugged. "There will be more fighting. Who knows who will finally win? We must take one day at a time."

"As we have always done, my son. The Lord has not made us prophets."

"But we can discern the times, Father. The Romans will not give up so easily. And the Zealots—they will never give up until they are killed."

Matthias seemed restless, and Joseph knew that his mind was not really on the political or business implications of their situation. After a moment of uneasy silence, Joseph asked, "What troubles you, Father?"

"You are my only son, Joseph—my only child. A day will come when you will have to choose. You are young. The Zealots will conscript you for the fighting. If you refuse, they will simply kill you, perhaps all of us. It is a foolish war, for no purpose as far as I am concerned. But what about you? You must decide where you stand. You must put your heart on one side or the other."

"I could certainly not fight on behalf of Rome. What do you mean? There are only two sides."

Matthias shook his head, frowning. "I do not state my feelings well. Look beyond the Zealot attacks, Joseph. This is said to be a war of principle. It is supposedly a fight to

90

rid all of Judaism of the influence and oppression of Gentile powers. The incidents about which the Zealots rave and the Moderates seek compensation, they are really nothing. It is a war of hatred. The Romans want to make us Romans; the Jews want to destroy the yoke that binds them to a king not of their choosing. But the unsettling thing to me is that no matter what one believes, it doesn't seem to matter. No, if there were only two sides, it would be fine. Jew against Gentile, that would be easy. It is Jew against Jew, so many factions—and the Romans are not much better. So I believe you must set your sights on the future, have a goal that will see you past the time of insurrection."

Joseph nodded. "I will try, Father. You are right, I have only been watching the wars from a distance, as though they did not really concern me. Tell me, whom do you believe to be right?"

Matthias sighed deeply. "How I wish I knew. I am a Jew. I want what is good for me and my family. The Romans bring a measure of peace and protection. We have prospered. And yet—"

"What?" Joseph waited silently, searching his father's face. He felt insecure but equal as he and his father together sorted thoughts and defined issues.

"We are Jews!" Matthias exploded in a tone nearly angry. "We were never meant to be governed by Gentiles. God Himself has chosen us, but for what? To die for the likes of Simon ben Giora? Or for Eleazar and his mad, grand ideas? I do not believe that this war is a national one. It is only personal. I am confused, Joseph. I do not understand what has brought us to this point, or what must be done to take us out. Perhaps that is why I side with the Moderates. Though we get nowhere, at least we do not kill people."

Matthias was silent, brooding, and Joseph, realizing that there were no answers, left him alone in the room.

He stood gazing at the rain falling into the open court-yard, and, like his father, tried to decide what it meant to be a Jew, what the war was really for, and where his sympathies lay. Across the city a mere mile away, other men had died trying to humble Rome. One day, perhaps soon, they would demand his help.

Alexandra came into the room and was startled by his quiet presence. She gasped. He turned, knowing that it was not Miriam.

"*Shalom*. The rains have come at last," Joseph said quietly.

"Yes, praise God."

"Have you heard? The Romans are gone. Simon ben Giora attacked them at Beth-horon and they scurried away in the night."

"You sound glad."

"Of course I am! It's a victory for Jerusalem." He watched her face and tried not to smile as she looked intently into his eyes, then smiled herself.

"You know it wasn't, Joseph. You're baiting me. I know that Simon wins victories only for himself." She shivered a little and said, "Do you think he's mad?"

"Perhaps. They tell me power does that to people."

"Sometimes I think Jerusalem would be better off if the Romans would win and occupy the city. Caesarea was peaceful enough."

"You haven't been there lately. There has been a great deal of fighting. It's everywhere."

"But not here, in the Matthias villa. I can never thank you all enough for allowing me to stay here. Had I joined my Christian friends, I am sure I would have fared poorly. God is keeping me through this troubled time."

"He keeps whom He will. Still, He gives us decisions to be made."

Alexandra did not question him about the decisions of

his mind, but Joseph wanted to tell her the things that were important to him to see if she would accept his answers, or add insight. "I may have to go and fight with the Zealots myself."

"Do you believe in the Zealot cause?"

"I don't know. I don't know if anyone really knows what the Zealot cause is. But I may have to fight, nevertheless."

"You have said that God keeps whom He will."

"And also that decisions must be made. My father and I have only just now been speaking of it. My father did not say it out loud, but I know what he wants."

"And what is that? For you to fight here in Jerusalem with Eleazar?"

Joseph evaded the statement, hardly hearing it, so intent was he on his own thoughts and on wondering what Alexandra's reaction would be. "Alexandra, do you know the law of the Jews?"

"Only a little."

"Married men—newly married men—are not conscripted for warfare."

She was silent again, and this time Joseph found the silence maddening.

"Don't you see? I could marry, and I wouldn't have to fight."

She turned away from him. "What is it you want me to say, Joseph? That I want you to marry Miriam and preserve your life? Or that I would rather have you die than marry now? Tell me, Joseph, what you want to hear, for it is not for me to say anything to you. I can have no choice where you are concerned, none at all."

In that moment they both realized that the stifled words and avoided glances had failed to quench love. There it was, obvious to both, but neither dared to grasp it, for indeed this love was cruelly barbed with complications.

She turned, and the distance between them was like the

Temple wall. Then Joseph knew the feelings of Roman generals throughout Judea, for nothing would have pleased him more than to find an opening in that wall so that he could get to the woman before him. But she stood in her world, and he stood in his, two people with no discernible future. Decisions! His heart ached with the decisions he must make, the things he wanted and could not have.

"Alexandra, you are so much a Jew. You follow the teachings of a Jewish rabbi. Why is there so much between us?"

"There isn't much, really. If you would follow Jesus too, there would be nothing at all between us."

"Or if you would stop believing that He was more than a rabbi. There is only one Lord."

"And only one Messiah for the Jews. I believe that Jesus of Nazareth is that Messiah."

"But what can that mean to you, Alexandra? You are a Gentile."

"Let me answer with a question. As a Jew, would you follow the Messiah if He should appear?"

"Of course. There would be no question."

Alexandra continued, "And why would you follow him?"

"The Messiah is the entire hope of all Israel. Messiah will restore Israel to its rightful position, 'purifying the sons of Levi.' He will establish the throne of David forever. There will be no more wars when Messiah conquers the Gentile powers." He looked at Alexandra, watching her face for traces of offense, but there was none.

"Joseph, we Christians believe that Messiah has already come, that Jesus of Nazareth was the Messiah. Many Jews have believed in Him and found in Him all the promises they hoped for. And we who are Gentiles, by God's mercy have been allowed to partake of the promises to Israel because we accept the Messiah."

A protest rose from Joseph's heart, but from his head

94

a fragment of Scripture blocked the haughty words. The reading of the prophets that was so much a part of his boyhood training returned to him. *"Sing and rejoice, O daughter of Zion: for, lo, I come, and I will dwell in the midst of thee, saith the LORD. And many nations shall be joined to the LORD in that day, and shall be my people."* Did Zechariah mean to say that there was room in the circle of Jehovah's arm for more people than Israel? Joseph remained silent, distressed.

"You are upset," Alexandra stated. "There is no need. Listen, I will tell you something Jesus once said. Once a Gentile woman came to Him to ask for healing. Jesus told her that He had come to minister to Israel. 'It's true, I am only a Gentile dog, but all I want is the crumbs that fall from the children's table.'† Oh, Joseph, the crumbs from the table are a feast! The Lord has enough blessings for all. The Gentiles will take nothing that rightly belongs to Israel. Does God forget His promises?"

"No, of course not. But—" He turned to Alexandra, troubled. "If I have missed Messiah's coming—where is the Kingdom? What is this war?"

"I'm not sure. I can only tell you what I know, Joseph. I am not a Jew, and I never had hope for a kingdom. All I know is that Philip told me that because Jesus died, I could be righteous in God's sight. I believed. And I am changed."

Joseph resolved to spend more time listening to Uncle David to see if he could find out more about the claims of Jesus. But his concern slipped away as he enjoyed his conversation with Alexandra, and his only wish was that his life would not change, that he might be as content as he was at that moment. They talked of their families, their hopes. The rain stopped, and the sun cast long shadows across the courtyard.

*Zechariah 2:10-11.
†See Matthew 15:22-28.

95

"Joseph, it will soon be time for the evening meal. I would like to find your mother and help."

"But there are servants," Joseph said, wanting her to stay.

She smiled. "It is a courtesy among women. And I am learning, too, along with Miriam. Joseph, Miriam will be here soon."

The significance of her statement crushed Joseph as he realized how much more he wanted to spend time with Alexandra than with Miriam.

"Joseph, she's a lovely woman. I wish to be her friend, though she will not hear anything about Christianity. I hope—"

She stopped and Joseph urged her to finish her statement, but she only shook her head. "There are many things that I want for both of you—for all of you, as well as for myself. I talk too much. It is something I pray about often."

Joseph allowed her to go, knowing that because of Miriam she felt uncomfortable spending time with him. How could he feel so close to this Greek, who was so removed from him in so many ways? One thing he understood all too clearly: to leave Miriam for the war was one thing; to leave Alexandra was another.

10

Nero Claudius Caesar Germanicus loved to visit Greece; and Achaia, the southern land, was Greece at its best. Today the imperial entourage, with its officials, warriors, wise men, and women, had left Athens and was visiting the rugged and barren island of Salamis on the Aegean Sea. It was a rare, happy day for the still youthful emperor for two reasons: this was the monarch's thirtieth birthday, and he was standing on the island near which the Greeks defeated the Persian navy and paved the way for the eventual routing of Persia from Greek soil.

Nero looked with appreciation over the waves of the Aegean. Laughingly, yet with seriousness, he said to Statilia, his statuesque wife of not yet two years, "I love victory! That is why I love this stony island."

"A message for your Imperial Worship," came the voice of a Greek messenger boy, who bowed low to the ground as he spoke.

"Give it to me, lad. Hurry." The boy delivered the message and scurried away as one of the group of surrounding officials tossed him a coin.

"Aagh!" came a gurgling cry from the collapsing emperor. Immediately his attendants rushed to his side, only to hear the Pontifex Maximus of Rome whisper, "My celebrated Syrian Legion has been utterly defeated and put to flight by the Jews. Now the whole empire will rebel against us, seeing that the Jews can annihilate one of Rome's finest legions." Like a man pursued, his eyes darted left and right. "It is a terrible omen to receive such news in this place of victory. The gods are surely angry."

His entourage stood about in uneasy silence, waiting for the emperor to initiate action. Finally Tigellinus, Nero's nefarious and shrewd counselor, stated candidly, "This weakness will be the signal for Vindex in Gaul to revolt against Rome, and Hither Spain may soon follow."

"What shall we do, Tigellinus?" Nero whined in the cowardly voice so characteristic of his reaction to anything adverse.

Tigellinus replied with calculation, saying, "The Jews of Jerusalem and Palestine have to be crushed swiftly in order to display to the distant barbarians who might consider revolt that Rome is still all-powerful. You must commission your best legions to destroy Jerusalem, tumbling its every stone to the ground."

The decision made, Nero demanded, "Whom can I send to save the honor of Rome?"

"Send my father and myself," came the immediate reply from a handsome soldier in the crowd of courtiers. It was the husky voice of a tall, clean-shaven Roman of high rank, indicated by the golden epaulet on the left shoulder of his white toga.

Tigellinus leaned over to Nero as the black-haired soldier approached. "Harken well to this one, Caesar," he whispered. "I think his father is our answer."

Titus Flavius Sabinus Vespasianus, as he came toward Caesar, was only twenty-eight years of age; but while serving with his father in Britain, he had proved himself to be an able commander. His name was identical to that of his father, the great general, but everyone called him Titus and his father Vespasian.

Titus was no less a soldier than his father. Though he had served in fewer battles, his knowledge of warfare was superior. And like his father, he knew people and could lead.

Still, the shadow of his father was not always a blessing.

Titus longed for an opportunity to distinguish himself personally, apart from the exploits of his father. Not that his father was against Titus' distinguishing himself, but it seemed that they always served together. If they could serve together in Palestine, however, surely there would be enough territory to cover to warrant two leaders—two generals—who might make great names for themselves and, incidentally, for Rome.

"O Imperial Majesty," began Titus, and Nero impatiently waved him to get on with his address, "my father defeated the Britons in a great war and thus gave your own father, Claudius Caesar, a triumph to celebrate. Vespasian is only fifty-eight now, a good age for a general, and he could cause you also to celebrate an even greater triumph by maintaining your authority in Jerusalem."

Nero nodded approvingly and, looking toward his waiting entourage, said in a voice edged with fright, "Yes, this talk of triumphs is more pleasant than the news of a defeated legion." Then, turning once more to his chief counselor, he said, "Tigellinus, cause the proclamation to be written that General Vespasian shall be made commander of the Roman armies of Syria and North Africa, and that he shall take their legions and crush the ingrate Jews. And be sure that the survivors of the Twelfth Legion participate in this war, so that the barbarians may be given to understand that our fulminata will be victorious in the end." Then, furtively, he added, "And what else, Tigellinus, ought we to proclaim?"

"Your Worship, we ought to make it clear in your letter commissioning General Vespasian that Rome does not merely desire a victory over the Jews. A victory will put down the Jewish rebels, but it won't stop the Gauls, the Britons, the Teutons, and the barbarians of Hither Spain. What we need is a triumph that utterly wipes Jerusalem from the map! Only such a total victory will teach the barbarians that the penalty for attacking a Roman legion is utter destruction of their homeland!"

"Yes, yes!" shouted Nero with insidious glee. Utter destruction of their homeland! Let that be the cup that we will make those Jews drink as their celebration for defeating that fool, Cestius Gallus. So let it be written!" He then declared aloud to all, "Pass out the wine to everyone, and help me to celebrate. I am sending the seasoned and victorious General Vespasian—and his son, General Titus— to avenge Rome upon the Jews, who treacherously destroyed our Twelfth Legion. It's settled! Drink with me to the inevitable victory of Vespasian and Titus."

A cheer went up in the form of a toast, "To victory! To Rome!"

Titus, his breathing already accelerated with excitement, bowed politely as he quietly backed away and out of the cheering crowd. He wanted to start packing at once, and he wanted to make the necessary preparations for leaving Greece and sailing to Palestine. The peace of Rome had not yet settled on the whole earth. There was at least one more war in which he could fight. He had a good feeling. Soon he would be beside his famed father once again, helping to organize the countless cohorts into a united force whose imperially assigned purpose was "the utter destruction of the Jewish homeland."

At last, in the month of Shevat (February), in the year now called A.D. 67, the Roman sea captain judged that winter was sufficiently spent so that he could sail, with Titus aboard, from Achaia to Alexandria, Egypt. Titus set about performing the tasks assigned to him by letter from his systematic father. Within days the previously alerted Fifth and Fifteenth legions were ready to embark on the broad-sailed Roman merchant ships, called "swans," levied from the harbor of Alexandria.

At Ptolemais, that great, ancient battle city with its

treacherous harbor, the remnant of the Twelfth Legion stood waiting. Anxiously they watched the horizon for the appearance of the tall sails of the Roman swans, knowing that the ships carried the soldiers who would replenish their ranks and give them the strength to return to Jerusalem.

Among the soldiers there waited a gray-haired general, the moving force behind this reconstruction. Vespasian watched the sea for the arrival of his son, whom he had commissioned to organize the Fifth and Fifteenth legions from Alexandria. These two legions, together with the famous Tenth (the Praetorian Guard) and the remainder of the Twelfth, would make a force of eighty thousand men, not counting the cohorts of equestrian cavalry and work forces for hauling baggage and siege engines.

At last the shout was heard. The ship was in sight, the first of a long line of vessels propelled by wind and slave labor, men captured from all over the world and set to work in Roman galleys.

It was a proud moment when the young and muscular General Titus embraced his somber and lean gray-haired father. Titus was full of news of Greece, the condition of the emperor and his women, and his passage from Egypt. But above all, his thoughts were in Jerusalem.

"Will it be difficult, Father? We have a huge army now."

"They have spirit, these Jews. Never underestimate them. Who knows what the gods have in store? Bad weather is to their advantage—illness, too. We must plan and work carefully, but today I make no boasts."

"You are too humble," Titus said, mildly reproachful. "No army on earth is a match for this force, commanded by this general. And the Jews are not even an army."

"But we have more than military status to consider, my son. They love their God, and they hate Rome. Love and hate are powerful allies—and to us, powerful enemies."

101

Titus was once again silenced by the judgment and insight of his father. He felt that perhaps, after all, he was not quite ready for fame. He thought of his own comments as he had ridden away from the harbor region with his father earlier that day.

"Father, you really should ride a better animal," he had said. "A gray mare—and a small one at that! Is that all you could find here?"

"Cestius Gallus had a reputation for making a great appearance on a large black stallion, but he lost his legion and today everyone despises him. I prefer to concentrate on winning the war; and if I am victorious, Caesar will not ask me what color horse I rode. We must focus on the important things." He had smiled at his son, understanding the enthusiasm of youth. "You are younger, my son. You and the legionary generals can ride on stately mounts, but don't pester me with anything unless it contributes to defeating our enemy."

That evening, in a building made into the temporary headquarters of the Roman army, Vespasian introduced his commanders to one another. But the introductions were interrupted by the arrival of two very important people.

Vespasian brightened noticeably as the man and woman entered; and after a brief welcome, he introduced them to the entire staff. "Let me present at this time the ruler of Galilee, Perea, Batanaea, Trachonitis, and Aurantis, our esteemed ally, King Herod Agrippa II. We are privileged to have you here with us. Please favor us with your observations on the situation in Palestine."

The stiff-looking Agrippa began explaining how he had pleaded with the Jews not to revolt against Rome, but every soldier in the room, no matter how old or how disciplined, found it nearly impossible to concentrate on the king's address. Eyes wandered, though faces remained politely for-

ward. The king's patriotic and correct message was no
match for his dazzling sister, the queen.

This nearly middle-aged woman with red tresses piled
high on her head was like a jewel in the desert. She bore a
look of dignity that betrayed none of the controversy
that surrounded her. And her delicate beauty, it was rumored, surpassed that of Venus. An audible sigh escaped
from one young man, but he was never disciplined for it.
He received only sympathy from those who sighed inwardly.

So this is the famed, or ill-famed, Bernice, mused Titus.
Suddenly he felt self-conscious that he, a general, could not
control his attention any better than his men. There she sat,
apparently enraptured by the king's speech.

Married to her brother, formerly married to her uncle,
she also had many other men in her life; she was both a
strict Jew and a friend of Rome, both beautiful and terrible—a woman full of contradictions. And, Titus had to
admit, ultimately desirable. Moreover, in his preoccupa-
tion with the woman, he noticed the look that passed between her and Vespasian.

At last King Agrippa finished and Vespasian announced
that food and wine were in the adjoining hall. Then he
closed the meeting with these words: "Remember, these
zealots are wild and insane with victory. They have already
defeated one imperial legion. I cannot allow them to defeat
another. We will fight this war in the best Roman style.
We shall destroy the cities of Galilee. We shall conquer
Samaria. We shall level the towns of Judea and Idumea to
the south. And, finally, when we have subdued all of Palestine and cut every supply line, we will surround and besiege
Jerusalem itself. We will starve the city to death, then assault its towers; and at last we will totally destroy the city
and level its walls to the ground. It will take us from two

103

to four years, but this step-by-step attack is the only sure way to guarantee victory to us, prevent the loss of another legion, and obey Caesar's charge to us—namely, that we bring about 'the utter destruction of the Jewish homeland.' "

The generals and Romans arose, shouting, *"Vale! vale!"* to the supreme commander. Only King Agrippa of Galilee and his red-haired sister held their seats, both looking grim. Other equally bold plans had failed.

The following months went according to Vespasian's studied plan. During Tivet to Tishri (January to October) of A.D. 67, Vespasian and his legions destroyed city after city that had joined the rebellion against Rome. (Those cities that surrendered immediately were spared, except for the symbolic pulling down of a lone wall or tower.) And to his other victories, General Vespasian added the favor of Queen Bernice.

11

As the days wore on and news of Vespasian's progress traveled south, Jerusalem became more acutely divided into parties than ever before. The Zealots were the party for all-out war against the approaching Roman armies, and were directed by four men: red-bearded John of Gischala, the crafty leader of the Galilean Zealots from the north; the more prudent Eleazar, head of the Jerusalem and Judean Zealots from the south; young, inexperienced Josephus, commander of the Galilean cities; and Simon ben Giora, dubbed "The Tyrant," who had ambushed the fulminata in the Beth-horon passes, leader of the Brotherhood of the Sicarii. The Sicarii were little more than assassins; they were named for the *sica,* the short knife used for night killings. Based in the south in Idumea, Simon ben Giora and his Sicarii stayed out of Jerusalem, knowing that they were not welcome there, and made periodic raids north. Also, those formerly called Pharisees backed the Zealots.

The Moderates, upon seeing the utter destruction of the fortress cities of Galilee and the leniency given to those cities which did not resist, wished still to preserve their city by suing out a peace. They were encouraged for peace all the more by seeing that Titus graciously spared the city of Gischala despite the treachery of John. At the head of this Moderate group were the high priest and the older men of the city. Those formerly called Sadducees were counted within this group, as was Joseph's father, the respected Matthias ben Joseph.

"Father, look," Joseph declared with a sweeping gesture that encompassed his surroundings. "I am surrounded by women."

"That is bad?" his father replied, grinning.

"Yes, in more ways than one."

The two men worked at sealing the barrels near the presses where laborers extracted olive oil. The sun touched servant and master alike, and all worked with rolled sleeves and robes loose and flowing, except when it hindered movement. Joseph watched the children running among the adult workers. They wore light tunics and seemed unaffected by the heat. He envied their carefree expressions, their innocent laughter.

Joseph had been talking with his father about the approach of the Romans and how it would affect their trade. Though his father began devising plans to export the oil, Joseph's mind was not really on work.

Matthias continued, "You regret not joining the Zealot forces?"

Joseph shook his head, frowning. "I'm embarrassed, that's all. I seem to be the only young man left in the area."

"And the other reason? You said being surrounded by women had many drawbacks."

Joseph avoided his father's gaze. "You know."

His father nodded. "I believe I do. You are caught in a love for two women."

"Or love for the wrong one." Joseph sighed. "Sometimes I feel—I don't know—that it's *all* wrong." He was quiet a moment, then said, "I've decided to join the Zealots after all, Father."

Without looking, Joseph felt his father stiffen and halt his activities. He knew that his father wanted an explanation.

He faced his father. "It is nothing against you, Father.

The Moderates are right. And they are wrong. And the same is true of the Zealots. But I'll go mad unless I act. Right now the Zealots are acting, and I will join them. That is, with your permission."

"And if I say no?"

"Of course I will obey."

"With whom will you fight? Eleazar?"

"No. I wish to go north to John of Gischala."

"But why? With Eleazar you could be here in the city, even live at home."

"I know that." Again he turned away, color rising in his face; but his father's familiar silence would not let him escape.

"It's the women," he said at last, exasperated. "I find no peace. I must get away."

Matthias toyed with the signet ring; he was quiet and thoughtful. "Perhaps I made a mistake in asking Alexandra to stay. She is really more to you than a pretty guest with new ideas."

"Much more."

"You know she can never be your wife."

The laughter of the children bounced between the two men. Joseph made no reply.

"She will never be wife," Matthias repeated. "If you do not choose Miriam, well. But you shall not choose Alexandra. Why go to war? What is the advantage? Time and distance will change nothing."

"But death might, Father."

"You mean you would rather die than choose between them?"

"Not exactly. But it is a trial. I have made a vow, Father. I have asked the Lord God for a sign. Last Sabbath, when I took the new lamb to the Temple alone, I swore before the Lord that if He brought me safe again to my father's house I would announce my betrothal to Miriam."

"When will you go?"

Joseph shrugged. "Soon. Will you speak to Mother?"

Matthias nodded and returned to his work, afraid. The busy sounds of his success were nothing if he had no heir.

Joseph left for Gischala in Galilee with only the briefest of farewells to both Miriam and Alexandra. Though he did not show Alexandra a preference in his words, he could not hide a certain look of longing. As he rode north, he thought over the past weeks and months when Alexandra had been in his home and the way she had influenced his family. She spoke of her Christianity only when asked, and she was polite but firm when questioned. Uncle David was so interested that he had even begun speaking to her personally. Joseph was not aware that his Uncle could speak Greek well enough to carry on a conversation until one day he happened upon Uncle David challenging Alexandra with portions of the Law and Prophets.

But it was certain that none of the family would be the same after this woman had entered their lives. Joseph's mother had come to look upon Alexandra almost as a daughter, for she had been eager to learn the ways of Hebrew women. Sarah grumbled openly about a mother who did not teach her own daughter such skills as grinding and weaving, but Alexandra simply accepted it, along with the occasional tongue-lashings that came to her. Occasionally she chafed under the ridicule and impatience, but even for that she apologized and did not try to cover her true feelings.

Matthias, though he tried to be indifferent and look at this woman as a political advantage, was always taken by her humor and her ability to tell entertaining stories about life in Caesarea. Once Joseph even heard him say, "What a pity she is not a man. What a leader she would make."

For Uncle David, she was the only known source of information about Christianity, the only person he had ever known who followed a person who laid claim to the Messiahship of Israel. Though he continually negated her claims, he found his arguments weak and unstructured, and especially ineffective in the light of Alexandra's rich inner life, which seemed to increase daily as the turmoil in the city became worse and worse.

To Miriam, she was an oddity, then an adversary, and finally a dangerous nuisance. Joseph wondered if Miriam understood his feelings toward them both, if they spoke of him when they were together. Alexandra had never spoken to him without invitation. She had never uttered a word of endearment, and the same was true of Joseph. Yet as he left the plains of Judea for the rugged north land, he knew in his heart that he loved her far more, in a far deeper sense, than he ever could love Miriam.

* * *

The "army" was little more than a band of thieves. They were ill-clothed, ill-fed, and too young, with an egotistical commander who cared little for his men. Joseph had to admit that he had been pampered, and he suffered for it while sleeping on the cold ground each night, cooking his own food, and caring for his personal needs.

He was distressed at the homage paid to John of Gischala by the younger men. Were they blind? Surely they did not believe that this man could make any significant impact against the Roman army. But many spoke of him with reverence, even awe. He was different, they said; he was above others. Joseph thought differently. He chafed at the orders and crude life, and he hated the warfare. Try as he would, he could feel no hatred for Rome. Without the improvements brought to Palestine by the Romans, Joseph and his father would be sitting in the market selling olives as his grandfather had done. When he aimed a spear or bow during the periodic attacks on Roman patrols, he tried

109

to shoot horses, and keep to the rear. And he counted the days until he should die.

*　　*　　*

Two months later, John of Gischala and his men came riding into Jerusalem, shouting victoriously, though they actually sought refuge behind the wall.

Joseph hurried to his own home, where his waiting family was eager to make him comfortable and hear his voice again.

"Tell us, Joseph," asked his father, "how was it with John in Galilee? Will you be able to stay long?"

"I won't leave Jerusalem again until this war is ended," he declared. "And I won't ever follow another Zealot leader. John is the best of them, and he is a liar."

"A liar?" exclaimed Matthias. "What has happened?"

"I see no way for our people to be victorious over the Romans, for they are more honorable than we are. General Titus laid siege to the city of Gischala, and as is his custom, he pledged to spare everyone alive if we surrendered. John told us we could not trust the word of a pagan, that we would be cut down like the Romans who left the tower here in Jerusalem. But that would not have happened, Father, I am sure. General Titus and his father have dealt with other cities in this manner."

"But what happened?" Uncle David demanded impatiently.

Joseph continued, reluctantly, wishing he could eliminate his own participation in the events. "John begged General Titus to lift the siege for one day in observance of our Sabbath, promising that no Jew would escape on so holy a day."

"And did the Roman do it?"

"Yes. Titus commanded all his army to back away from the city, and he said that he was doing it to honor our God." He carefully avoided the eyes of his father and uncle. "But

110

then, John—" Joseph paused, obviously ashamed. "John ordered all of us to mount up on horses, camels, mules, anything available—on the Sabbath, mind you. Then he gave us a speech. He said, 'Titus will spare the women; it is we men who must flee to save our lives! Besides, if the Romans rape and kill our women, we must remain alive to get revenge!' "

"He broke his word? And the Sabbath as well?" Uncle David was shocked.

"Yes. We rode like madmen for Jerusalem, leaving Gischala to the Romans. Many of the men hail him for it. But I'm ashamed of it, and so are many others. I'm ashamed of running away, and ashamed of John."

"Then you really did ride away with the others—on the Sabbath?" cried Uncle David.

Frustrated and angry, Joseph replied, "And should I have disobeyed and been killed?"

"But it was wrong—"

"And it is wrong to kill and fight and disobey. What is to be done, Uncle? One sin brings on another."

Uncle David was quiet now. "The Law makes no provision. There is something missing." He turned to Alexandra, who sat next to Miriam, listening to the conversation of the men. With a crafty gleam in his eye, he asked, "Tell us how Jesus of Nazareth would have solved this riddle. What should be done? Should the law of the Sabbath be broken, or should Joseph have disobeyed his commander and been killed?"

"Oh, Uncle," she replied, smiling. "I know so little of the laws of the Jewish people. All I know is what those who knew Jesus have taught me. He was often accused of breaking the Law, but actually He only ignored the impositions made upon the Law by men. I suppose, if He were here, He would tell us that the Lord God established the Sabbath for the good of mankind, so that we might rest and

111

worship. It is always right to do good on the Sabbath. Evil is wrong on any day of the week. As for me, I think Joseph did the right thing. God will judge John for causing others to sin."

"Good!" cried Uncle David, surprised and happy. The answer pleased him, though he was embarrassed to admit it. It reminded him of the way he had felt about God as a child—that Jehovah loved him and was interested in him. Later in life, God seemed to be looking over his shoulder, waiting to catch him in an error. Was that the essence of the teachings of the Nazarene? Did he believe that the Law should help instead of hinder? *Why,* Uncle David wondered, *at this late time of life, am I suddenly confronted with so many choices? Perhaps it would be better simply to follow in the way of my fathers and ignore this carpenter's son? But what if—*

Alexandra came to him and asked, "Uncle David, is it possible for one to keep the whole Law?"

"Yes—no." He hesitated a moment, then, "I have never known anyone who did, but of course that is why we make sacrifices, to atone for transgression."

"May I tell you something, Uncle?"

He nodded, and she went on. "I believe that Jesus was the one person on all the earth who did keep the Law in its entirety. It was possible only because He came from God the Father, and was God's own Son. But though He was perfect, He died apart from God, as a curse."

"Child, I do not understand. You speak in riddles."

"Some time ago Joseph took a young lamb to the Temple as a sacrifice to God. Tell me, had the lamb broken the Law, or done any wrong?"

"No, of course not."

"Then why did the lamb die?"

David paused, making sure of his answer. "Sin brings death. It was so before the time of Moses. The lamb was

112

a substitute for Joseph, that the Lord God might not require the man's life for the man's sin."

Alexandra nodded. "Did you ever see John the Baptist, Uncle David?"

David shook his head. "No, I have heard of him, and knew at the time that he was hailed as a prophet.

"As Jesus came to him one day, John said, 'Behold the Lamb of God which taketh away the sin of the world.'* Do you see what John said that Jesus has done for us all?"

Her earnest tone and submissive attitude made David quell any harsh words he might have spoken to the young woman. She obviously wanted only good for him. And the thought was interesting. A perfect man might give his life for another, but for all others?

"You give me much to think about, Alexandra."

"You are gracious. My thanks for listening to a simple woman."

Later, in the kitchen, where Sarah ruled over any man present, David sat humbly waiting for food. Sarah scurried about, not allowing the servants to prepare anything for her brother. She chatted nervously, concerned about her son and the unstable condition of her whole environment.

"David, I'm afraid to leave this house to go to the market—even if there were anything in the market to buy. Three days ago both Levias and Sophas ben Raguel were clubbed to death while walking together in the lower city near the king's garden! Everyone knows that the Zealots did it because both of them had branded the Zealots as 'murderers of the prophets' a few days before." She kept talking as she stirred vegetables and heaped them onto a plate.

"Oh, David, talk some sense into Matthias before it is too late. The rabbis say that the Christians are misled, but Alexandra tells me that the Christians are already leaving

*John 1:29.

113

this city. She said that their Jesus prophesied before He was crucified that Jerusalem would be destroyed because it rejected His claim as Messiah."

Uncle David could listen no longer. Her words affected him less than the aroma of the vegetables. "Hurry, woman! I am more concerned about my empty stomach than Jesus of Nazareth." She brought him the food, and he said, "It doesn't take a self-proclaimed Messiah to prophesy that Jerusalem will fall, Sarah. Don't be too concerned over such words. I also heard that the Galilean prophesied that He would return some day and save Jerusalem from invading armies. Why aren't His followers waiting for their Messiah to come and rescue them today from the Romans? What is Messiah, anyway?"

Sarah shot back, "Since you were a child you always had an answer for everything. I may not know enough to answer your riddle questions, but I am smart enough to know that the Nazarenes are doing the wise thing in leaving this cursed city!"

Uncle David arose and pronounced, "Jerusalem is a blessed city, the city of Adonai's Temple!"

"No," replied Sarah in an instant, shaking her finger under her brother's nose. "It is an accursed city where the Sicarii stab people by night and the Zealots club decent men by day in the Temple precincts, and the Romans wait outside the walls to devour us all!"

"Blind woman."

"Stupid, bigoted *holy* man!"

"Sarah! You must not—"

Uncle David was interrupted by a shout at the gate, and soon a young servant of Matthias was admitted.

"The Zealots have chosen a new high priest," he announced. "They said that none of the living former high priests would do. They declared that the Holy One, blessed be His Name, would Himself select the high priest through

114

the casting of lots among the men of Jerusalem. Then after countless casts, each time eliminating half the men gathered in the great court, the lot fell to a young farmer, visiting Jerusalem from a village named Aphta. His name is Phannias ben Samuel. No one ever saw him before."

His eyes wide with fury and indignation, Uncle David stood up. He seized the messenger by the shoulders and demanded, "Name the tribe! Is he of Levi? Is he a Hasmonean or of the Aaronic-Zaddoc lineage? Tell us, boy!"

The boy pulled away, frightened. "He is neither Levite nor Hasmonean. They say that he hardly knew what the priesthood was, for this was his first visit ever to Jerusalem."

Uncle David ripped open the brown robe that he was wearing and threw back his head and sobbed. "The kingdom is again taken from Israel. The Zealots this day have partaken of the sins of King Jeroboam ben Nebat, dividing our kingdom and creating their own religion!"

As Uncle David began to wail and chant, the boy told more. "Ananus and Jesus ben Gamaliel, the two former high priests, were in the Temple treasury openly denouncing the Zealot leaders for what they had done. They named both John of Gischala and Eleazar as the enemies of the Lord. If you go quickly they may still be there—if the Zealots have not murdered them."

Uncle David stumbled for the door and ran northward through the streets of the upper city toward the Temple. Panting and sweating, he at last arrived to join the crowd.

"Look, standing on the wall of separation," someone said, pointing.

"It's Ananus, the former high priest. Shhh, he's going to speak."

The loud but strained, high-pitched voice of the elderly high priest soon struck their ears. "It would have been better for me if I had died before I saw the house of the Lord filled with so many abominations. John of Gischala and

115

Eleazar ben Simeon are not Zealots. They are tyrants who murder and kill whom they will, and now they have even revoked the priesthood commanded by God, blessed be His Holy Name."

The crowd responded, in a low, muffled set of voices, "Blessed be His Holy Name."

Ananus continued, saying, "Oh, the bitter tyranny we are under—and you people have made it so by overlooking these tyrants' sins one after another. Even if it costs me my life, I say to you that we must rise up and put an end to these tyrants who perpetrate such evil as murdering their enemies even in the sacred Temple courts themselves. These beasts are no better than the Roman idolators! They slay our elders, they delude our women, and now they have set aside the priesthood and defiled this sanctuary."

The partisan crowd could hold its peace no longer. "Amen, Amen! Death to the tyrants! Death to John and Eleazar!"

But Uncle David, so filled with indignation a few moments before, suddenly knew that the decision was wrong.

"Eye for eye," he quoted to himself as he mingled with the crowd, listening for reactions, hoping to find another who felt as he did. *"To me belongeth vengeance," God had said."* *There is so much law,* he thought. Even the lawyers themselves could not tell just which law applied in certain situations. But something inside told him that Ananus should have accepted and waited for Jehovah to destroy the violators, those who offered this strange fire. The something inside—the unwritten laws. Could it be—Jesus of Nazareth had once summarized the whole Law into two brief statements—love God and love others. That was not Ananus' interpretation, nor Uncle David's. Was God merciful, or was He just? Was love the quality not stated in the Law of God but manifest in the work of God? Throughout

*Exodus 21:24 and Deuteronomy 32:35.

116

his life, David had been considering his feelings toward God. He had not thought of God's feelings toward him.

He went home to puzzle and ponder anew the intricacies of Jehovah. As the sun set, he lifted his face to the crimson clouds and asked, "Have You revealed Yourself to this Greek woman, but not to me? What have I left undone? What is it You want? Obedience? I will give it. Love? I will give that, too. And sacrifice, and service, and tithes. But show me. Show me, for what I have now is not enough."

12

The dust cloud of the twenty thousand Idumeans who came from the southern desert blew toward the south walls. Old and tired high priests climbed the ancient stone stairs to join other citizens of Jerusalem on the top of the wall that was directly beside the Valley Gate.

"Why have they come?" asked Joseph. "The Zealots hate them. For whom do they bear arms?"

Matthias shook his head. "They come to help the Zealots, never doubt that. But something of their plan is amiss. The priests have shut the gates. They cannot get in."

Joseph felt a tremor, as if the air carried the hatred from the Idumeans to him. Beside him Uncle David leaned far out to the edge of the wall, hurling the words of Moses toward the approaching hoard. "Cursed shalt thou be in the city, and cursed shalt thou be in the field. . . . The LORD shall cause thee to be smitten before thine enemies."*

As the minutes wore on, the first representatives of the Idumean army became visible as individuals. They were dressed in dirty gray tunics and carried bows and swords. They went down into the sides of the south rim of the Hinnom Valley, into the place known as Gehenna. Here, with swords in hand, they pushed their way through the burning garbage of the city with its eternal fires, and then reappeared at the north rim of the valley, knocking on the closed and bolted Valley Gate. More and more of them kept coming, like a locust plague. Soon over two thousand of them were impatiently waving their swords below and outside the high, ancient south wall of Jerusalem.

*Deuteronomy 28:16, 25.

118

On and on they continued to descend into and then ascend out of the great valley, congregating under the shadow of the mighty limestone ashlars of Jerusalem's south wall. Within an hour after the first contingent had arrived, the crowd of Idumeans from the red land of the Dead Sea had swelled to four thousand.

After another two hours, it appeared that all four of the loosely organized Idumean legions had arrived, each consisting of about five thousand men and having its own commander. The mass of men gradually spread out to encircle the entire southern portion of the city (also called the lower portion). The uncontrolled Idumeans began hammering with their swords at both the Valley Gate at the southwest of the city and at the Dung Gate on the southeast. With no siege engines, however, their random beating on the gates did little damage except to further fan the fires of resentment against those who had barred their entrance.

At last some order was reached and the dialogue between the high priests and the Idumean captains began. The Zealot leaders and their forces, according to their own treacherous design, were nowhere to be found during this initial stage of negotiation.

Simon ben Cathlas, a burly, fifty-two-year-old, half-Jewish Edomite, was the leader of the Idumeans. He signaled for silence among the ragged soldiery and then began to shout up to the former high priests.

"Jerusalem is the 'common city' to all in Israel," he called. "You have no reason to lock out the Idumeans from such a holy city. It belongs to us also."

"Where are your sacrifices?" replied Ananus. "Do you come to worship, or destroy?"

A rude shouting reaction erupted from the throngs of soldiers below, who were infuriated over being shut out of the city. After some noisy minutes, quiet was once more restored.

119

"If we were Romans you traitors would open the gates and greet us with garlands of flowers!" cried Simon.

"We are traitors? What about John and Eleazar, who disregard God's laws and choose priests as you might a goat in the marketplace? Did they not call you here to kill and burn in this holy city?"

A new wave of hooting began in the Idumean ranks, and the two high priests, in disgust and despair, disappeared from sight.

"It's a ruse," declared Matthias. "Simon and Eleazar have at last united against the Moderates. They have hired these people to destroy us and then help them against the Romans. But they have tried to make it appear that the idea originated with the Idumeans." Then in an anxious voice he said to his brother-in-law, "David, we must go immediately to secure what we can of our trade and supplies. This will be the end of any peace in Jerusalem."

Together they moved through the crowd and descended from the wall, racing against time and the circling army below. The Romans to the north, the Idumeans to the south, the Zealots within—Matthias knew that the time had come to make the house of Matthias a private fortress.

They went first to their own house, breathless with the urgency of their mission.

"Sarah," Matthias cried as they entered the house. "Quick! Gather some food and come with us. We have many errands to run. Miriam! Alexandra! You must come too. Bring as many servants as there are in the house, and we will go first—"

"Matthias! Matthias! What is wrong? Why are you shouting so?" Sarah stood frowning at him.

"Why are you standing, woman? We must bring everything we have under this roof—now, within the hour, if possible. Do not antagonize me by standing there," he shouted at her. "Obey, if you are my wife!"

120

"Matthias, I only—"

"Do as I say!" he shook her by the shoulders. "Gather food and follow us to the olive yards." At the sight of her tears, he quieted a little. "Sarah, Sarah, I want only to preserve you through what I know will come. Help me, please. We must hurry." For a moment he looked at her intensely, then he suddenly hugged her to him, hard, then stood back. "Joseph is bringing the animals. Uncle David has already gone to marshal the servants. Bring the young women and help."

"Yes, Matthias," was all she said. Soon they were quick-stepping through the city once more, this time toward the Matthias olive yards, carrying baskets, collecting vessels along the way as curious neighbors watched.

Alexandra and Miriam walked together but did not speak until Alexandra fell, cutting her hand on a sharp stone. Miriam helped her up and helped her collect her baskets and the wrapped food she carried.

"You should be more careful," she said coldly.

"How touching that you care for my comfort," Alexandra retorted. Again the silence resumed, and, as usual, Alexandra's heart began to burn with shame and sorrow at her cutting remarks. *I should apologize,* she thought not looking at Miriam. *No, I would only be rebuffed; Miriam does not want my apologies. Miriam wants only one thing from me, and that is for me to leave the Matthias home. She hates me.* And a thought arose that Alexandra tried to deny but could not. *I have begun to hate Miriam,* she thought.

Alexandra looked carefully at the path, knowing that if she looked heavenward she would feel the glance of the Savior, knowing that He would be unhappy with her. The rebellion welled in her heart. Miriam had been unkind to her, disdainful, haughty. But she knew that the real reason for the bitterness she felt was the presence of Joseph in their lives, and that the jealousy she felt toward Miriam was really bitterness toward God. He had given Joseph to Miriam although she—Alexandra—would certainly have been a better mate.

They trudged along through the hot morning when others were resting. Alexandra was alone, alone as always. Her family did not understand her new life and did not care to understand it. Friends and home were far behind, and she now dwelt in a land of strangers who swept her into their destinies but not into their hearts. The one who loved her in Caesarea, she cared nothing for. And the one she loved here could never be hers.

At last they reached the olive yards, and as they entered the cool shade Alexandra seemed to sense her Savior interrupting her life, as He so often did, with love. As she set about collecting the olives, she thought of Him praying alone in Gethsemane and she saw the look on Philip's face as he told with shame how he and the others had deserted Him. Jesus had been alone—in a strange land, with His true home far behind Him, in a world He was not part of, knowing that He would soon die. Still, she harbored the hurt, refusing to give it up to Him. But here on the hillsides overlooking the city where He had lived and taught, she could not relegate Him to some distant heaven. As he had done with the apostle Paul, He seemed to meet her face to face, demanding a decision.

Is this why you brought me here, Lord? she asked silently. *Have you brought me all this way, through all this, to learn more about You—how You lived and died—alone?* It was what she had wanted, but she had thought that it might be easier. There was no other choice. Eventually she swallowed hard and went to find Miriam to ask her forgiveness. Alexandra expected no solace, and she received none.

The sun hung dangerously low when Matthias told every-

122

one to stop working and return home. They packed all the olives in baskets, barrels, the assembled vessels, and the women's shawls. The strange caravan began to move toward the upper-city villa. The servants and pack animals would not come this way again. The fruit left behind would be for whatever army came this way first. The presses, the barrels, the immature trees—Matthias ben Joseph glanced back only once, wondering just how much he would be able to give his son, then set his face toward home. He thought of orders not filled, of customers establishing trade with other merchants because of the war, and the weight of his years nearly crushed him. He could never begin again.

Joseph marched along, guiding a small donkey that was pulling a cart much too heavy for the poor animal. He saw Miriam, smiling benignly, and he clenched his teeth, biting back the scorn. Had she no eyes, no ears? Did she not realize that all they owned they now held in their hands? He knew that he should be flattered. She had complete confidence in him and in his family; she trusted them all to care for her. It was lovely, but unwise. His eyes strayed to Alexandra, but he would not let them linger. It was no use.

They reached home just as darkness settled into the courtyard. They locked the gate behind them and began unloading their burdens. They worked silently, each one too tired and afraid to communicate with the others. When the animals were finally stabled and the house full of fruit and oil and exhausted people, the hush of midnight crept over the house, and they slept.

At nightfall the Idumean army was still locked outside of the city, unable to join the Zealot leaders. All over the south half of the Zion slope, outside of the Valley Gate at the southwest and the Dung Gate at the southeast, they sat in huge clusters, swords and shields in hand, complaining bitterly and threatening what they would do if they ever gained entrance. Then the night began to chill and light rain started to fall.

What had been a drizzle developed into a healthy rain, and rumbling thunder could be heard periodically in the distant west. Most of the thinly clad Idumeans who had previously sat or lain on the dry, brownish yellow dirt now stood, trying to find some shelter, or at least a more comfortable position.

Three hours after sundown, the sky seemed to break open and the rain fell in torrents, with bright sparkling flashes of lightning and roaring crashes of thunder cracking all around the Hinnom and Kidron valleys. Every Idumean held his shield over his head because of the rain and used his free hand to shake his sword at the city, hating the high priests and the traitorous Moderates who had locked them out in this downpour. Thus they passed the night, their hatred rising as the noisy, howling winds and cold rains increased.

An hour after midnight many of the Idumeans started to debate whether this misery had befallen them as a judgment of God for coming armed against the holy city. There was talk of returning home, but news of a change quickly replaced that thought.

The sound of a saw could be heard from the Dung Gate! Word spread quickly that the Zealots of John and Eleazar who were within the city had captured the nearby Dung Gate. For some mechanical reason they had to saw through a huge wooden bar to release the gate, but as the anxious thousands waited, they saw the huge, ancient gate slowly open in the drizzling darkness. The Zealots beckoned for their cheering allies to enter for what was now to be the "liberation" of the city from the Moderates. Soaking wet, terribly angry, the men from the red lands entered by the thousands and began a torrent of death.

With solemn and terrible vengeance they worked their

way through the city, rousing the sleeping Moderate population, who opened their tired eyes to see their murderers at hand.

Gradually they found their way deeper and deeper into the city, killing and plundering as they went, burning and looting in a strangely quiet mob.

Stray bands broke into homes and looked for food, money, and women, sometimes going methodically from house to house, sometimes searching and destroying at random.

From her place in the upper room, a sleepless Alexandra spied the marauders. Quickly she hurried to wake the sleeping household.

"We must all hide in the cellar," Matthias instructed. "Perhaps they will think we have fled the city. I am sure there are none who know us personally."

Together they climbed down under the floors and waited.

The man who approached the Matthias villa was tired and hungry. He had been unaccustomed to killing before this night, but he was finding it strangely satisfying. He got a boost from a passing comrade and scaled the wall, heading directly for the house. He shouted, "Come out, or I'll kill you when I find you."

When there was no answer, he went in. Empty. *But the gate is locked on the inside, he thought. Someone must be here—a servant perhaps, left behind to guard the house.* He walked cautiously, looking in corners, watching the shadows. After a short tour, he decided that the main part of the house was vacant and flopped down on a mat to rest. But as he closed his eyes and drew a deep breath of satisfaction, the sweet scent of a woman's perfume met him. He turned over and realized that the mat was a bit warm. Somewhere in the house, the woman must still be hiding!

He got up cautiously, alert again, and began walking back and forth until the sound of his steps took on a different tone. He went back, walked again to find the exact spot, then pulled up the door violently.

"Come up, or I shall come down and get you!"

Below the occupants held their breath, huddled in the darkness.

"I know someone's down there. When I come I'll send my sword ahead. I don't care who you are. If you value your life, come up here."

Everyone stifled a gasp when someone moved in the cellar. It was Alexandra's voice that called, "All right. I'm coming."

Tears sprang to Matthias' eyes and he clenched his fists. *Lord God, why had she done this?* he cried inwardly. *What will they do to us all?*

The Idumean smiled with delight at the dark curls, the solemn, dark eyes, and the lithesome body of the pretty Greek as she appeared in the room. She climbed out and carefully closed the door behind her. "Now," she asked politely, "what is it you want?" She smiled at the man, and he could hardly believe his luck.

"Want? Why, food and companionship, of course. What does any lonely soldier in a strange city want?"

"I thought as much," she said brightly. "I felt in my soul that you would not be like the others who came. They were—rude, very rude to me." She frowned petulantly. "Come," she said, her tone brightening. "I'll get you something to eat. I think the others left something."

"What others?" the man demanded. He grabbed her arm, drew her close. The scent was the same as that which had come to him from the bed. Perhaps she was alone in the house.

"Why, the other soldiers. Aren't you a Roman?"

"No. Don't lie. The Romans are not in the city."

She looked at him, wide-eyed. "No? He looked Roman, with his sword and shield and breastplate, and that lovely helmet with the feathers. He was very handsome, but not interested in me. The other nine who were with him, though—"

"Ten Romans?" the Idumean looked warily around. "How could they get in? Only ten? I've seen none since we entered at midnight. How long ago did they pass?"

"Shortly, only about half an hour ago. If you look, you might find them in the stable." Too late she realized her mistake.

He laughed out loud, spun her around, and pushed her toward the kitchen. "Ha! You thought you would get me away from the house so you could scamper to the neighbor and leave me all alone again? No, no, I've found the most lovely creature in all this miserable city, and I mean to enjoy you. Now get me something to eat while I decide just how I will celebrate this occasion with you."

Alexandra choked back the tears, her back to the Idumean. She must try again. She only hoped that the rest of the family would not try to help her and perhaps cause a disturbance that would bring more of the mercenaries into into the villa. She chattered nervously while she got bread, cheese, and olives for the man, whose eyes never left her.

At last he interrupted her. "Where is the rest of the family?"

"Oh, gone to the hills," she replied, and not too quickly this time. "They left me here to feed the animals, as it is of no consequence whether I live or die."

"What? As pretty as you are? Surely you are promised to the firstborn son."

She shook her head. "Only a servant." She saw the cloud of doubt shadow his face, and quickly she spoke to him in Greek.

"You are not a Jew!"

She shook her head. "I told you, only a servant, purchased in Caesarea. My family was poor, we had—"

He rose and came toward her. "I care nothing for your past—or your future, for that matter. Come here."

She hesitated. "But you have had no sweets or nuts—"

"Come here." He took her hand, pulled her to him, and drew her along beside him through the house, making one last check for other people. Suddenly there was a slight cough, and the Idumean released his hold on Alexandra for a moment as he spun around. In a moment she escaped into the courtyard and headed for the stable.

"Come back," called the Idumean, softly, lest he draw the attention of his comrades. Seeing his prize escaping, he became less cautious. Joseph killed him when he stepped outside the door.

He found Alexandra shivering in a pile of straw. "Alexandra," he said.

She cried aloud, not knowing who called. Then realizing that the person had called her by name, and finally recognizing the sound of his voice in that one word, she flew into his arms, sobbing and laughing.

"Shh! Quietly, my love. The danger is not yet past."

"Joseph, Joseph! I never heard you come from the cellar. When did you leave?"

"I never went down with you. One cannot fight with the Zealots even for a day and learn nothing of strategy. It was foolishness to send all of us into the cellar with no escape route. But I could not say it to my father. I simply stepped out during the confusion."

"You were there, in the house, all the time?"

He shook his head and drew her closer. "I waited near the gate. The Idumean came in at the rear of the courtyard. I didn't know he was in the house until I heard him laugh. I knew immediately what you had done. How could you—"

She pulled away from him, all the time longing to stay, and never, never go back. "We must tell your family. They will be afraid for me."

The meager light of the descending moon came through the stable window and glistened on her cheek where the tears still trembled. The tiny beams of light were like fairies that flitted away, mocking him with promises of what might have been.

They called his family up from the cellar, and together they watched the wall until morning.

Heaps of bodies could now be seen by the light of dawn. Dead and wounded lay strewn all around the Temple environs, their blood staining the hallowed stones. Eight thousand five hundred Jewish Moderates were slaughtered by their kindred from Idumea. So fierce was the work of these "rescuers" that they killed in this, their day, double what Gessius had slain in his—all to save the city, all done in the name of the Almighty.

The Zealots who watched them leave were the victors. The plan had worked, though the events had come in a strange and haphazard sequence. So few Moderates remained alive that, by virtue of number, the Zealots held the city.

But power was too great a prize. John and Eleazar, rivals in all but name, vied for prominence, and soon John began his own reign of terror against Eleazar and his followers.

The Romans had only to wait for the city to devour itself.

13

Animated voices came from the ornately furnished, large scarlet tent of the Roman commanding general. The tent was pitched just north of Gophna, a Jewish town in Benjamin's territory of Judea which had just surrendered two days before. Gophna was only twenty miles due north of Jerusalem. The target was well in view when startling news came to the council of generals.

"Nero is dead, stabbed by his own knife, and Galba is emperor," Vespasian declared to an audience of shocked leaders.

General Sextus Cerealis, sixty-one and the oldest commander present, spoke immediately. "This will mean civil war. Galba is disliked by many of the commanders, and they will never permit him to be emperor without a fight."

"And what of our war here, Vespasian?" asked another.

"And what of you?" questioned a third, as he motioned toward Vespasian himself. "The whole army knows that you are a thousand times more fit to steer Rome than that cowardly, mean-tempered Galba."

Vespasian raised his hand, fingers spread wide. "My fellow generals, choose your words. If Galba truly is the emperor, and we have no cause to doubt the report, then an unwise word heard by the wrong ears could earn you a treason charge and death when you next return home to Rome." Though he spoke to the generals, he watched the guards.

As he continued to speak, the other men calmed down and listened. There was not a man present, however, who

130

did not think that Vespasian was more fit to rule than Galba. Each man was by this time experienced enough to know that the scepter more often than not did not fall into the most able hand, but rather into the hand that happened to be free to catch it as it fell.

Vespasian raised his wine glass for a traditional and appropriate toast.

"Hail to Galba, the new emperor of Rome!"

"To Galba," all murmured, rising. They stood on a tightrope, and no one dared step boldly. Galba was weak. Too much show of loyalty would alienate one from the forthcoming emperor if Galba should fall. Yet they knew that if Galba became strong enough to hold the throne and purge his enemies, testimony of this ceremony would not only save their lives and careers, but might also bring them promotion and honor within the new administration. Only the quaestor, fiercely loyal to Vespasian and more emotional than the hardened veteran generals, made an openly unhappy face as he toasted the new imperator.

As they returned to their seats, Vespasian continued to expand on their new situation. "All of you know that we had planned within the next week to march all of our four legions to Jerusalem and commence the siege that would successfully end this war. For the last eighteen months we have been working toward this very target—Jerusalem. We have isolated Jerusalem from its northern support by subduing all the hostile cities of the Zealots in Galilee and Samaria. We have isolated Jerusalem from its heartland—namely, from the sea coast of Joppa, and from its surrounding territory of Judea and Idumea. Today, except for some small towns in Judea, only two fortified mountain cities, Herodium and Masada, defy us, along with Jerusalem herself.

"We are at last prepared for our third campaign. We will pluck Jerusalem like ripe fruit, ready to fall. The city today is shut up; no one goes in or out. Everything in Palestine is ready for the attack. Even the Qumran caves to the south have been cleared of those Essene fanatics by cohorts of our Tenth Legion."

"Hurrah, we still march against Jerusalem!" shouted the quaestor.

"No," replied Vespasian in a quieting voice, with no hint of rebuke. "Everything is ready for the attack—except two very important factors. One, the Jews have now begun to fight a new civil war, and in my judgment it is folly to attack an enemy at any moment except when he is at his weakest point. That point, we now realize, has not yet arrived for Jerusalem. I do not want to attack the city now and unify the Zealots. No, we will let them slaughter one another, and then at their weakest moment we will begin the siege.

"But second, I am hesitant to commit our armies to a full-scale conflict against a foreign city when the fate of our own home city stands in doubt. Once a siege of a city the size of Jerusalem is begun, we cannot, on a day's notice, decide to pull out the legions and ship them off to another location. Thus, as long as the fate of Rome wavers and as long as the Jews smite each other within the walls, we will keep the bulk of our legions in a state of readiness here in the Judean regions."

The quaestor sighed aloud, "Ready for what? To defend Galba?"

The general continued, disregarding his quaestor's words. "I am sending General Titus to the new emperor today. He will take him my greetings, pledge him the loyalty of each of our four legions, and await his instructions as to the continued prosecution of this war. Meanwhile, my generals, keep your legions ready."

Then with a familiar nod, Vespasian dismissed the commanders, adding to his salute the barbed words, "To Galba."

With questionable enthusiasm all repeated, "To Galba," and left the tent. Vespasian was alone with his son.

"Must I be the bearer of false words, Father?"

"Of course not. As long as Galba is emperor, he deserves the protection of his own army."

"Other commanders feel differently. I could name some who would give that allegiance to you."

"That is their decision. I care nothing for Galba, only Rome."

Titus was as usual impatient with his father's reasoning. "Why don't you use these legions, and the others who would support you, to overthrow Galba right now?"

Vespasian wore his usual look of calm dignity. "The Jews have a saying among them: 'Let another man praise you, and not you yourself.' If I rule, it will be decided by those other legions. They will come to me."

"Why don't you go to Rome and give Galba your message personally?"

There was no reply, and when Titus followed his father's preoccupied gaze, he saw Bernice entering the general's personal quarters.

Titus turned scarlet, jealousy and embarrassment churning within. "I see," he breathed, and turned away, still in his father's shadow.

Within the day he started for the port city of Joppa, from there to glide across the sea on one of Rome's swiftest three-sailed swans. Once on its voyage his vessel would be urged on through the windless hours by the singing lash in the galley below, a galley whose many empty seats had been recently replenished by captured Jewish boys who had been providentially saved from the coming massacres of the Judean campaign. The delicate hands that only days ago in freedom rolled the Torah scroll open now pulled oars of slavery as the new master slept in pillows of ease above. Thus the Roman craft sped through the waters westerly, rushing an anxious Titus to a rendezvous in Rome.

In Jerusalem, food became scarce as the civil war continued. The family of Matthias ben Joseph fared better than most during the struggle, but they did not live in the ease to which they were accustomed. The servants were nearly all gone, having run away to fight under their chosen leaders. Crops could not be completely harvested, and roving bands of soldiers raided the fields. The supply of silver remained, but at last it too began to shrink as prices soared.

The villa remained secure, isolated from the atrocities of the civil strife all around. But the strife affected every decision, every thought of the day. Staying alive became the major goal of the family.

Simon the Tyrant, who destroyed the Roman Twelfth Legion, had reappeared outside the city and clamored for entrance for several days. At last the Moderates of the city decided to use him as the Zealots had used the Idumeans. They let him into the city, planning to make use of his assault, not realizing that his own personality and power would make him yet another threat. So the civil war branched out, and Eleazar, who held the Temple courts in the eastern quarter of the city, was besieged by John of Gischala, who held the lower city in the south, who was in turn besieged by Simon the Tyrant, who held the upper city on the west.

Matthias remained in his house with his family until it was necessary to find food. Then he took Joseph or David to see what could be found. The markets were empty, and it was foolish to walk there. Instead they went to the homes of the wealthy to bargain and trade, oil for meat, well water for vegetables, sometimes money for goat's milk or grain.

"I believe Simon will be the one to reach this part of the

134

city first," Matthias stated as he and Joseph returned from food gathering. "He is anxious for the possessions of the wealthy. As soon as he can break past the Zealot lines, he will be here."

"Perhaps the Romans will return soon and rid us of them all."

Matthias smiled impishly. "Oh, ho! You sound as you did months ago. Is Rome our friend again?"

"Perhaps not, but Rome would be the fastest solution to the problem."

Matthias gave an indifferent shrug. "They have failed before."

"Not this time. You have not seen them, Father; nothing like this army has ever come against Jerusalem before." He paused, then said, "This is not over for me, you know. I must return soon, or I will be executed as a deserter. It is only thanks to the poor administration in the ranks of John of Gischala that I remain at home."

Matthias replied, dismayed, "But you said you were through with John of Gischala! How can you fight with such a man?"

"It is not what I would choose. I believe I can hide a little longer, and when the Romans return—for they will, I know it—then I shall do what I can to defend Jerusalem against them, and try not to think about whom I am fighting for, except myself and my family."

"How strange. You will fight those who you think are doing their best to end this intolerable situation."

Joseph nodded. "It is a time for doing strange and contrary things that have no reason and no meaning." Bitterness was evident in his voice, and it was not missed by his father.

"You are speaking of your vow. You regret it." Joseph was silent, and his father said anxiously, "Joseph, you must pay! Did you think the Lord would wink at such a vow?

135

'Better is it that thou shouldest not vow, than that thou shouldest vow and not pay.' "*

"I know, I know, Father. But—the payment is nearly more than I can bear! I really believed that I would die in battle and would never be faced with the decision. Father, I love Alexandra!"

Matthias walked on steadily, eyes lowered. "I know that. But it does not make anything different. You have promised. Even if you had not made the vow, Miriam expects you to fulfill the intentions you have indicated through the years."

"But if I had not vowed, would I have been allowed to marry Alexandra?"

"It is a foolish question, Joseph. Who can take back the past? But no, you would not."

"Why?"

"She is Christian. And she is Greek. It would not be wise for you."

"Jews do not always marry Jews. Even the prophets—"

"Joseph," Matthias exploded, "it is done! You must fulfill your commitment to the Lord. Do not make yourself more miserable by thinking of what might have been. Is Miriam so hateful to you now?"

"No," Joseph answered thoughtfully, "she will be a good wife. But," he sighed, his heart heavy beyond description, "to see what might have been, and to settle for what is, that is hard, Father."

"When will you complete the betrothal?" Matthias asked in his business voice.

Joseph looked closely at his father to try to see if he understood or cared, but the older face betrayed nothing. "Tomorrow," he answered.

That night, as the sun began to set and the air cooled, he

*Ecclesiastes 5:5.

136

saw Alexandra leave the courtyard to go to the well, and he followed her.

"Alexandra, I must speak to you."

Other women were going to the well, and Joseph guided Alexandra away from the main path, toward a small grove of trees, where he said, "I have spoken to my father. Miriam and I are to be married." When she did not respond, he went on, filling the empty air with words. "I wanted to tell you myself. I made a promise, a vow. The Lord has saved me alive from war, and now I will marry Miriam. Do you understand?"

"I understand that you would have married Miriam even if there had never been a war. Joseph, you must not apologize. She will be good for you. It is the right thing to do."

"Alexandra, how can you tell me that? How can you look at me and pretend that you don't know that I love you more than Miriam?"

"I know that. Do you think it has been easy, living here with your family, learning your ways, being part of you in so many ways, and knowing that you would marry Miriam?"

In reply to his startled look, Alexandra said, "Yes, I love you. And I have never said that to any other man. Though you are not a Christian, I do love you. But Joseph, if you were free to marry anyone you might choose, and if you would choose me, I could not say yes."

"But why?"

"Because my life belongs to Jesus, the Christ. Unless you were willing to make such a commitment, we could find no harmony in our lives. We would be like a plowing team made up of an ox and a goat, hearing commands differently, living by separate rules, looking at life from different points completely. We would soon hate each other. I am new as a Christian, Joseph, and I once told a man that I

137

could not think of loving anyone who did not also love my Lord. But I have a choice whom I marry."

"Then it does not matter," Joseph said, his voice empty. "The vow made no difference."

"Yes, Joseph, it was a good thing. The will of the Lord is very clear. But how I wish—how I pray—that you and your family would see Jesus as your Messiah—the Messiah of the Jews."

"I am sorry, Alexandra, but I cannot. I try and I will continue to examine the evidence. Right now, I see only war. I do not believe this is the world of the Kingdom."

The two looked at each other, alone as before. Then Alexandra lifted the water jar. "I must go to the well. It will be dark soon."

Joseph nodded, his throat tight, and walked toward his home as she went toward the well. They would not speak again.

The next morning, Miriam stood in the door of the Matthias' upper room. After her initial fear of Alexandra's beliefs, she had come to respect the other girl, but she refused to speak of Christianity. Although she had known for some time that the man she had always expected to be her husband had lost his heart to this woman, something deep inside told her that she would still be the mother of Joseph's children.

"Joseph is speaking to my mother," she said. "Today he delivers my dowry." Alexandra nodded, but did not speak. She was feeling, at that moment, that God had certainly given her a burden too great.

"I am leaving, Miriam," Alexandra said gently. "The city is open to pilgrims now, since the Romans are quiet. I will go back to Caesarea, to my family. The city there is peaceful."

"Alexandra, I am not as happy as I should be." Miriam came into the room and spoke as though she had not heard

138

Alexandra at all. "I have waited and waited for today, and sometimes wondered if Joseph was displeased with me because he waited so long to arrange our betrothal. But now I feel—disappointed."

"Why is that, Miriam?"

Miriam shrugged. "I suppose it is because he loves you more than me."

Alexandra made a move to speak, but Miriam silenced her with a gesture and continued, a note of sadness in her voice. "I love Joseph. I have loved him from childhood. I never loved anyone else and never wanted anything except to be his wife. And I will be. But I wonder—how would it be for us if you had never come to this house?"

"Oh, Miriam, I never meant to bring you unhappiness."

"You have not. Joseph will be a good husband. I will have a dozen children, and when we are old, perhaps he will not remember you as much, or as often. But you will always be there with us."

"Miriam—"

The girl smiled slightly, acceptance in her face. "You had no plans to love Joseph, I know. If you had, could I speak to you now? With all your strange ways, you wished me only good. But Joseph is mine. I am not sorry. God must favor me. I am a Jew and I will marry him."

Alexandra forced back stinging tears, praying in her heart for relief from the pain of loving a man who was unavailable, and from the pain of coveting the joy of a woman so deserving. At last she shook herself free and said, "Look here. I have something for you. A present for your wedding."

From among her own jewelry she took a square of fine purple cloth and unfolded it. Inside was a pair of earrings, pure gold, shaped like tiny strings of almond blossoms. Miriam accepted them, then shook her head.

"I never have anything for you," she said. "You have

given me gifts, and I cannot repay."

"Then it is truly a gift. Miriam, please wear these when you and Joseph are married. And think about Jesus of Nazareth when you do. He, too, gave a gift that cannot be repaid. As a lamb, He died. Though He had no sin, He took our sin upon Himself that we might find favor with God. Oh, do think of the Christ when I am gone."

"I will. And I would beg you to stay, except that I know you would be unhappy." Alexandra listened, but heard no note of triumph. "Will you leave before the wedding?"

"Yes. Who can tell how long the Romans will remain so lazy? I must travel quickly. Other Christians are traveling, and we will leave before Passover, while the gates are open and the Romans allow pilgrims to come and go."

"Then I will tell you good-bye now. I will be in preparation for the wedding and I will not come to the house again until we are married. Peace to you, Alexandra." She turned and was gone, and Alexandra, alone in the morning sun, sat quietly meditating until her shadow disappeared.

Then she began to gather her belongings, and while the family of Matthias ben Joseph rested in the midday heat, Alexandra left the villa and went to the road to await the group of Christians with whom she would travel. At last they appeared in the shimmering heat, men and women whom she had found at the Temple, where they worshiped God without sacrifices. She had joined them in private prayer times, and she had sung the new songs of praise and adoration with them. They had often met together, as was the new teaching, on the first day of the week. But as they went toward the edge of the city, carefully avoiding the encampments of warriors, she felt more lonely than she had ever felt before in her life, and she wondered why God continued to offer her delicacies that she could not accept.

14

Word had spread through Jerusalem that Galba, the new Roman emperor, had been stabbed to death in the middle of a Roman market after only seven months and seven days of rule. Otho was now emperor. Already, however, fresh stories of new trouble were reaching the east. Vitellius was rumored to have been chosen to be emperor by the legions in Germany guarding the Teutons, and it was rumored that soon there would be another civil war, Vitellius versus Otho.

The weeks of listening to rumors and awaiting news dragged by for Vespasian. With no fighting in Palestine and no news from Rome, he had nothing to do but wait and wonder. He drilled and marched his soldiers, keeping them ready for war, wondering if they would ever fight.

"I don't think I can take much more of this," he said tensely, peering through the tent door, then pacing back and forth.

Bernice sat on a large cushion, arms around her knees. "It is dull. Have you heard from Herod?"

"Do you mean when he will return? No, I know nothing except that he was wounded and that he recovered. Nor do I know the whereabouts of my son. I am a man on an island."

"With me," Bernice teased, and pulled him down beside her.

The messenger, as he had been instructed by the guard, listened until the conversation resumed inside the tent, then coughed and announced his presence.

"Otho has committed suicide after being defeated by Vitellius. Vitellius is the new emperor," the messenger said.

"How long?" demanded Vespasian.

"Otho reigned only three months and two days."

"Weeks ago! Vitellius has been emperor for weeks while I sat here on the plain like a wingless bird!" He strode about his quarters, muttering, then called in his generals.

"We will resume the campaign. Galba, Otho, now Vitellius." He shook his head in disgust. "Let him fight his own battles. We will march against Jerusalem."

The generals eyed one another, waiting for the spokesman.

"No," declared Cerealis forcefully, "we shall not. We shall support you in a campaign against Vitellius, for you will be Rome's next emperor."

Before the supreme commander could protest, the leaders told him their strategy. They reasoned that they had fought greater battles than the legions in Germany, and surely greater ones than had many of the men in Rome who had not so much as left home soil. Why then should the Italian legions and those of Germany have the privilege of naming the next emperor—especially when everyone knew that the valor, experience, and fairness of Vespasian was vastly superior to that of the wild-living Vitellius?

Vespasian could not longer refuse, especially when he contemplated the coming abuses by Vitellius. So he himself formed an army out of the swiftest-marching five-thousand men of his four legions in Palestine and sent them under his loyal general Corso Mucianus to Italy.

"You are leaving, then?" Bernice asked.

"I can't expect to stay here while men fight for me in Rome."

"I shall be alone," she pouted.

"You, my lovely, will never be alone," said Vespasian, and kissed her good-bye.

By the time Vespasian had reached the city of Antioch in northern Syria, having ridden all night by horse, people were already learning of a great victory won by the eastern legions on his behalf. When the news reached Rome that Antonius Primus was coming to the city with his victorious eagle standards at the head of the triumphant eastern legions, another commander loyal to Vespasian and his many cohorts at once captured the Foro Romano, the stately capitol buildings of the Roman forum. Vitellius, however, attacked him and soon recovered the capital, killing the commander.

Within the next twenty-four hours, the eastern legions, led by Primus, began to approach Rome from the north. After great battles in three different locations, the power of the eastern legions prevailed and Vitellius' legions were routed thoroughly. The populace, charging Vitellius with being the cause of the civil war because of his many abuses, turned upon him, grabbed him, tormented him, and then at last, in a frenzy, beheaded him in Rome. Vitellius' reign had lasted eight months and five days.

Vespasian now reigned over the vast Roman spread of territories. He, however, did not for long forget the land to the east which he had left, and thus he quickly sent a dispatch to his son, now in Alexandria consolidating support for his father, to resume the attack against Jerusalem.

As spring erupted on warm, yellow-sanded Palestine, which was again beginning to turn green, Roman legionnaires could once more be seen marching everywhere on the roads. The world would learn that Rome, in spite of what happened and how long she was delayed, does not forget to avenge herself against a nation that has the temerity to destroy one of its legions.

The shrill blast of the last trumpet—always the third—and the Roman Fifteenth Legion began its sixty-mile march from Caesarea to Jerusalem. Behind it was the Twelfth, thirsting to cleanse its name from the defeat of A.D. 66. At the head of these two legions rode Titus, again on his immense stallion, his silvered breastplate shooting off arrows of light in every direction. His red-plumed silver helmet and crimson cape gave the supreme commander a dazzling majesty that he had never seemed to have when beside his father.

He had hurried from Rome, nearly giddy at the prospects of commanding the Jerusalem attack. He had been hailed by the soldiers and welcomed as an equal and respected as a leader by the other generals. Upon entering the commander's quarters, he made a quick decision. Calling for a scribe, he ordered, "Send a letter to Bernice." He would assume *all* the status of his father.

Throughout the country people presumed that the Romans were still preoccupied with their own civil strife and were no longer paying any heed to the holy capital of the Hebrew faith. Many of these Jewish itinerants refused to give credence to the rumors of a Jewish civil war being fought in the very environs of the sacred altar, with a Simon attacking a John who was in turn assaulting an Eleazar.

Only the followers of the Nazarene, "Christians" they were now called, were exiting from the city. They at once believed the stories of Romans being on the roads and marching toward Jerusalem. They cited warnings to flee which were from a book they called in the Greek *Evangelion kata Lukon,* the Gospel according to Luke.

On the thirteenth of Nisan (March-April), the day before the feast, the watchmen on the walls of the holy city reported to their respective leaders that the Romans had arrived in great numbers. This could indeed be called the first day of the siege, and the noise of the Roman hammerings and hackings could be heard from three directions.

Inside the city, Joseph married the woman he had promised to marry, and surrounded by armies on every side,

144

they spent a night together, quiet, each knowing that love was not the bond in the union.

The next morning Joseph rose early and went to his father. "I have paid my vow. I am returning to the fighting."

Matthias only looked at his son, not surprised. "Where will you be?"

"On the outer north wall."

"Umph! Like Uriah the Hittite. Because you could not marry the Greek, will you leave Miriam a widow?"

"It will be as the Lord God wills," he said, and went to say good-bye to his bride.

Again he lived among the rough followers of Simon and John, now somewhat unified against the Romans. Each day he wondered if he would live to see another. Beyond that, he did not think, and when the Romans had been pounding at the wall for eight days, Joseph hurried toward the upper city and his father's home.

"My husband," Miriam said, "you have come to me again, as from the dead."

Joseph responded coldly. "I have come to the safety of my father's house."

Miriam, rebuked, lowered her head and said nothing.

Joseph was at once sorry for his words. "Miriam, forgive me. I am preoccupied with staying alive. Perhaps one day I will come back to stay. Right now, I can only live a day at a time."

She nodded and smiled. Then she asked if she might serve him something, but her presence irritated him. He wanted to be alone, to rest from the sound of the siege engines, to smell the good smell of this home, and to forget the unwashed bodies and blood that assaulted his senses from day to day.

"Soon," he muttered to himself, "it will have to end soon."

He slept, and by the time evening came he was refreshed. He told his family of his experiences and was encouraged to find that they were still finding enough to eat, though meat had become practically nonexistent.

"Poor Uncle David," Matthias said. "He took only a dove for the Passover. Still, it was more than most."

"And was the Holy One pleased with such a sacrifice?" Joseph inquired. "It surely must have cost a great deal."

"Yes, it did," said his uncle in a faltering voice as he entered the room. "I hope—I believe He was pleased." Joseph was surprised at the muddled tone of his uncle, the troubled look about his usually stoic face.

"Uncle, are you unsure?"

"I am wondering at the ways of God these days, Joseph. Always, I have kept the Law. It was easy in the old days— well, easier than now. I brought sacrifices, I paid tithes. But times have changed and the Law has not. I am thinking of the time when—God forbid, I hate to say it, but if the Romans should occupy the Temple, then I could not sacrifice at all!"

Matthias tried to comfort the old man. "Our people have lived before with no altar, and we are still His people."

"I do not wish to be only one of His people, Matthias. I want to be righteous, like Abraham, or like King David, a friend of God, a man after His own heart. I want to know that God is pleased with me *always,* but—" He wrung his hands, the fear and uncertainty overwhelming him. "I live each day wondering, Have I done enough?"

That night, as Miriam lay beside her husband in the darkness, she asked him a question. "Do you believe as Alexandra believes?"

"Of course not. It is a Gentile religion, corrupt."

"I don't think so. Uncle David should be a Christian. He would know then that the Lord found him acceptable."

Joseph laughed. "By becoming as the heathen, the Lord

146

would be pleased? What nonsense."

Miriam shook her head. "Alexandra told me that we cannot possibly do enough to please God, to be acceptable to Him. And it is true. Uncle David has said so himself. If he feels inadequate, what about you and I, who are not nearly so careful about the laws?"

"You should not have listened to Alexandra."

"Well, I did. I was not married to you then, and even if you had commanded me to keep away, I might have disobeyed. She told me of her beliefs, and if she believes what she says, it must not be entirely wrong. She is a good woman."

"And how does Alexandra propose that one become righteous?" Joseph asked sarcastically.

"She believes that the death of Jesus was not an ordinary one, but that He died as a sacrifice for all of us, to cleanse us from sin."

"And that we sin no more?"

"No, but that if we take His death upon ourselves, God sees us as perfect. Like the scapegoat sent away into the wilderness, our sin is taken away by His death."

Joseph frowned in the darkness, somewhat irritated that he had no answer for Miriam. "It makes no sense to me. Speak to Uncle David, if you wish."

"I shall," she said, "if he will hear me."

* * *

After the siege by the Romans began, Uncle David felt more free to walk about, for the soldiers in the city were preoccupied with fighting. It seemed good to gossip with the other men again, if only for a brief interlude, and he found great joy in the social life.

One day, on such an excursion, he happened to meet a very old man sitting alone against the side of a building, staring into heaven.

"What are you looking at, old one?" asked Uncle David.

"I was wondering if, perhaps, Jesus of Nazareth might appear in the sky. He said He would. It would prove that He was a prophet."

"Did you hear Him say that?" asked David eagerly.

The old one shook his head. "I did not, but Matthew the publican, one of His followers, told me. I've been watching now for some time, since this fighting began, for Jesus also mentioned the destruction of the city, you know. I thought there might be a connection between the two events." For a moment he seemed confused in the way of the very old. "Sometimes I do forget," he said.

"Tell me about Him," David demanded, shaking the old man, who seemed to doze.

"Do you believe that He was the Messiah?"

"Perhaps," replied the old man. "Some said He was. Many believed it just before He died. I myself followed Him about during those last weeks. Certainly He did many miracles, but His teachings were strange."

"What about the Kingdom? If He was the Messiah, why has the Kingdom not appeared? Why did He die instead of reigning?"

The old man shrugged. "Some said it was because we Jews would not have Him. Some said that He always knew He would die, that He never intended to drive out the Romans. The twelve, you know, those who were His chosen, they say He will come again, and *then* He will establish a Kingdom. Who knows? I think about it often. I watch. Perhaps He will."

Uncle David left the old man. It was always the same. Those who had seen Him, like his own father and uncles, did not seem to be able to make up their minds. Those who had not seen him, like Alexandra and Joseph, seemed to have all the answers—but they were not the same answers. How he had pored over the scrolls these past months, searching for some clue. His own encounter with Jesus of Nazareth had been brief, and David had been a young man then, undiscerning.

He remembered a Sabbath, a day when he had been outside the city and had seen a crowd of Pharisees. There with them was Jesus of Nazareth, about whom he had heard, but knew little. He went to hear the conversation.

They were quizzing Him as to why He had been picking grain on the Sabbath, since that was against the Law, in their estimation.

The man replied that King David had done as much, and He made a startling statement, one that left the Pharisees speechless. "The Son of man," meaning Himself surely, "is Lord even of the sabbath day."*

What did it mean, "Lord of the sabbath day?" Uncle David went through the city, thinking of the information about Jesus he had been gleaning. He went past a building where he knew Christians met together often, and hesitated. He had heard that they had a written collection of the words of Jesus. But he did not dare go in.

*See Matthew 12:1-8.

15

"You there. Leave your bow and arrows here and report to the Tower Gate! Simon has ordered that we send two hundred men out to try to burn down the wooden towers in front of us. Otherwise the Romans may push them forward and breach the wall. They will supply you with a torch and shield at the gate."

Joseph's body numbed.

"Come on, get moving." He started toward Joseph, sword drawn.

"No, not him," Zechariah the wall leader intervened. "Not this one, Judah. He is married and is not supposed to be put on raiding parties!"

"Listen, Zechariah, Simon himself is married, and he doesn't slack from duty for fear of death!"

"They have told me that no married man has to go on a raiding party!" The two men faced each other, while Joseph shivered.

"No," Zechariah stated again, "this Joseph is my best bow shot. He killed a Roman on a horse from five hundred paces. I saw it myself. And besides, he *is* married."

"Then give me another man from your part of the wall."

"Take ben Sosas."

"Ben Sosas?"

"Yes, ben Sosas. You heard me."

"He's married too."

"Take him anyway."

"What will I tell him?"

150

"Tell him? You're a sector leader! Tell him nothing. But he is worthless on the wall. He does nothing but throw stones."

The recruiter walked on, muttering. Zechariah turned to Joseph and smiled.

"I, too, had a wife in my youth."

Joseph said, "You know I do not shoot well. Hitting the horseman was a lucky shot."

Zechariah shrugged. "It doesn't matter now. Don't question the good that comes your way."

Joseph nodded, but in his heart, he certainly did question. The next week, when the Romans broke through the outer north wall, ben Sosas died, and Joseph returned home.

He sat quietly with his wife in the darkness, close, but not touching. Miriam was alarmed at the pounding of Joseph's heart, but waited for his thoughts to be expressed.

"I've been unkind to you, Miriam," he said at last.

"That's not true."

"It is. And I—if I die, you must know I—had no intention of hurting you."

"Do you love me?"

Joseph hesitated, only an instant, before he said, "Yes, in my way, as only I can."

"Then why have you come home against orders to tell me your heart?"

Joseph said, "I have not told you my heart, really. But if I die, it would be wrong not to have said," he breathed deeply a moment to steady his voice, "that I am *truly glad* you are my wife."

"Would you not rather be married to Alexandra?"

Joseph smiled into the darkness. "Of course you would know." He rose and went to the curtained doorway, listening to the stillness of his sleeping family.

"I married you. I am not sorry. God willing, we shall live together for many years."

Miriam was quiet, and Joseph continued, almost absent-mindedly, "Isaiah Asher was killed when the Romans broke through, just as he feared. It was strange. Zechariah sent him off the wall to get him calmed down. Then there he was when that first giant stone gave way and slid and fell. The noise was indescribable. The Romans saw the wall break and cheered. They were through the opening in an instant, shouting like madmen. Their swords were swinging from side to side like wild Gathites. They must have killed a hundred men below us in the thirty seconds that I watched. Our men on the ground did not have a chance, because the Zealots were so sure—*so sure*—that the Lord would never permit the wall to be breached by Gentiles!"

"Please, Joseph."

"All right, Miriam. But tomorrow I must find Zechariah, that old lion, and thank him again for saving my life. Miriam, when I watched those Romans pour through the hold, I couldn't move. I was afraid—no, *terrified!* I'm always afraid."

"And Zechariah?"

"Perhaps he is afraid. Perhaps he is wise. He pulled at my arm and screamed at me, 'Follow me, Joseph! We can run south on top of the wall and get away!' Then he tripped and I helped him up and we both ran. Later, when we were safe, we laughed. We called each other cowards, and then heroes. But we are alive, Miriam."

"You must sleep, Joseph."

"So I will have strength to guard the middle wall tomorrow? I can only hope that the Lord will see fit to spare me again by another miracle. How long will He perform miracles to save me? Once more? Twice?"

"I am only grateful. I will not question His ways."

"But why us? Other women are widows tonight," Joseph said, angry.

"Oh, Joseph, I don't know. Shall we reject God's gift?"

A note of weariness was evident in her voice. "This war is so needless. I resent losing you because the Roman procurator and our leaders can't settle their differences. But God is keeping you through it. I cannot speak for others, only myself, but I am thankful to have you every day that you are alive. I love you, Joseph. I loved you when we were children together playing around your father's camels and dirty oil barrels. I waited for you even when—when you loved another."

"Miriam," Joseph said. His voice was stern as he returned to her in the darkness. "Miriam, my father's oil barrels were *never* dirty."

They both broke into laughter and hugged one another to stifle the noise, laughing out loud into each other's shoulder. Then, as the laughter softened, they remained, rejoicing in life.

Before dawn lighted the city, Joseph rose to leave.

"Joseph, I must tell you my heart as well."

"Yes?"

"I am a Christian. I have decided to follow the Nazrene."

Joseph said nothing for a full minute, then told his wife, "We shall speak of it later."

"But we may not have another time. I must know. Will you put me away?"

"Miriam, why? We have so much trouble now." He was exasperated, his joy forgotten.

"I had no choice. I believe He was the Messiah. I must serve Him."

"What do you know of the Messiah?"

"Little, I suppose, but I lived daily with Alexandra. She had peace, and love like no Jew I have ever known. I hated her, but she loved me, and though I was afraid at first, I finally saw that there was nothing to fear."

He snapped, "Not even the wrath of your husband?"

Her calmness surprised him. "No, for I have done what was right. Many have died because they love Him. And you will do what is right, Joseph."

He shook his head, dismayed. "I live daily in fear, and now my wife adds to my care. How shall I continue?"

Miriam waited, silent. "You had to know, Joseph."

"Alexandra!" he shouted into the dawn, and the name echoed across the stone courtyard and against the walls. "I could not have you, but I am still married to a Christian. You and your Christ! Can't you leave me alone?" He turned to Miriam. "I'm leaving."

"God keep you."

"There is *one* God. You have chosen another. Do not add blasphemy to your sin."

"My God is the same, Joseph."

Impatient, he turned toward the open window, hoping to avoid the rest of his family. "Good-bye, Miriam."

For the next five days the battle for the second north wall followed the pattern of that for the first. Roman engines continually by day and night hurled rocks at the defenders on the wall and smashed to pieces every building and hovel behind it.

Then came "Nico the Conqueror," an extra large battering ram swung back and forth by ropes. This spelled the end, as "Nico" performed its work of devastation and doom against the thick rocks of the wall.

After two days of relentless smashings, the pitiable middle north wall yielded. Once again the stones smashed to the ground, crushing anyone unfortunate enough to be beneath them. The second wall was now breached and the Roman infantry began to enter the Second Quarter of the city with swords swinging madly, partially out of hatred and partially out of fear each man had for his own safety. Each knew that only by killing the man before him could he escape being stabbed himself. In this hand-to-hand combat

154

even a moment's glance of sympathy for a fallen comrade could result in a sword being thrust into one's own stomach.

With the second wall broken, the citizens of Jerusalem withdrew deeper into the city, and deeper into their houses. Matthias ben Joseph entered his house, dispirited and dirty. He had spent the evening removing all valuable items from his house to a secret storage place.

"Close those upper shutters, Sarah," Matthias urged his wife. "I don't want anyone to see an oil flame coming from here. Anyway I can't listen to any more of the shouting. Anyone would think the Zealots had broken into the Roman camp from the drunken celebration outside."

"Well," responded Sarah, still peeking out of a half-open shutter, "Simon's men are telling everyone that the Romans have lost so many soldiers in the narrow streets of the Second Quarter today that they will never dare to enter again." Matthias frowned and sat heavily on a plain wooden bench, one of the few pieces of furniture remaining in the house. "Do you believe that, Sarah? The Romans are already in the northern parts of the Second Quarter. Within days they may break through and attack us here in our upper city."

Sarah paused, and then in a firm, realistic voice stated, "You are right. You are right, I know. The Romans have come too far to be turned back in the streets. They will come and come until they finish taking the Second Quarter. The city should surrender at once and be spared the death of all inhabitants. And these poor pilgrims! It is them I pity the most, those ignorant, pious ones who came to see the Temple at Passover, and who are now trapped with us." She peered outside again, and in a quiet voice, said, "I wonder what has happened to Alexandra? And to Joseph?"

"Joseph will stay on the walls, and run when he can. He will be all right. He will come home."

"Home—to what? Perhaps they will burn the house, and us. And, Matthias, Miriam is sick."

"Miriam? But she is young."

"Well, she is sick. She pretends, but I hear her cough and at night—"

"What is her disease?"

"Bad food, perhaps, or bad water. Death is everywhere."

"Well, we must buy time," Matthias said firmly. "We will hide in our tunnels after the Romans break into the upper city. Then in a few days, we will bribe them with our gold to let us live and to let us go free. Then we will begin anew as paupers, but at least we will be alive, and if that comes to pass I will be grateful."

Sarah tensed at her window seat. "David is back. He is coming to the door."

David ben Asher entered and placed an old cloth bag in the center of the room. He raised his thick finger to his stout lips for silence, and then spoke in an exaggerated whisper, "Shhh, even the walls have ears!" Then, pointing at Matthias accusingly, he warned, "Hold your tongue my brother-in-law. I heard what you said while I was at the door. Simon's men have orders from the Tyrant himself to slit the throat of anyone who speaks favorably of a surrender or a peace treaty with the Romans. They have already this night silenced the lips of more than one who spoke up. Beware, my brother."

Matthias, leaning forward and whispering back said, "That is because Simon knows that if the city surrenders the Romans will crucify him, and John and Eleazar as well. And he is such a fine deliverer-messiah that he would rather see a few hundred thousand women and children die if it will grant him another few weeks to live."

"Mmm, food," murmured Sarah, a little too loudly to suit Uncle David.

He frowned and motioned for silence. "The food situation is critical since the fall of the second wall. They store grain in the Second Quarter. Simon and John's men will break into any house where they think food is stored. They think that, as the soldiers and defenders, it is their right to eat first." His eyes gleamed roguishly. "I found this in an abandoned store in the Second Quarter."

"You, a looter, David?" sighed his sister in disbelief.

"I am not a looter!" David declared. "The merchants have abandoned the Second Quarter. They fear that the Romans will kill them. Why should the food be left to fatten the bellies of murderers? Besides," he added, looking a bit sheepish, "I left a note in the book saying what I had taken. I will make it right."

"David, the Holy One will bless you for what you have done," Matthias said. "You have risked your life so that we could have food. Some of this we can eat now; some of it we can save for when the famine gets more severe."

Uncle David nodded solemnly. "And we must share. So many are sick." The uneasy silence made him ask, "Are you sick, either of you?"

"It is Miriam. Not bad yet, but she needs care."

David nodded. "She carries many burdens. I will pray. Oh, if I could only get to the Temple, if I could only find a worthy animal to sacrifice!"

He paced about the room, frustrated.

"Here is a beautiful offering, David," said Sarah kindly, touching the bag of food, "as beautiful as the water from Bethlehem's well which King David poured out before the Lord. We will give food to Miriam, and surely God will be pleased. The bag is so big! And look at all that is in it. Vegetables and *meat*." She took charge of the large bag and headed for the kitchen.

* * *

During the next three days, Titus ordered cohort after cohort to pass through the break in the second wall, into the boiling cauldron of man-to-man combat within the Second Quarter section of Jerusalem, which lay between the middle

157

and inner north walls. Hour after hour the fierce struggle continued, with the Zealots slowly but steadily giving ground to the relentless and ever oncoming Roman hordes.

Zechariah and Joseph, as wall guards, moved back to the inner wall. This technical duty for the experienced sector leader and wall bowman spared them the gruesome task of engaging in hand-to-hand combat in the chaotic death struggle below in the narrow, camel-stenched streets and lanes of the Second Quarter—no-man's-land.

At last the cohorts from the Tenth Legion were stopped only by the third and last inner north wall and by the tall four-towered fortress, the Antonia, which guarded the sacred Temple hill itself.

The Zealots held it firmly and it was the final bulwark between Romans with fire and a Temple with flammable wooden beams and columns. Here Joseph stood from day to day, firing arrows at advancing Romans, until a friend arrived with a message from the upper city. *Your wife is very ill.*

Through the night he watched with her as her fever rose.

"Oh, Matthias," cried Sarah in the still-darkened morning, desperation in her voice. "Miriam is shivering and hot with fever. Joseph cannot be allowed to go back to the Antonia this morning!"

"Don't make the situation worse, Sarah," pleaded Joseph's father. "If Joseph doesn't arrive at the wall by sunup, and that's only an hour from now, they will send a squad of men to our house to kill him. The Romans brought ladders up last night, and siege machines. Simon promised death to any guard who failed to appear at his position this morning."

"Curse Simon!" seethed Sarah, with a grimace of hatred.

Joseph wanted nothing in the world except to cling to his sick wife in that quiet room. Instead, he went off slowly into the streets.

"They will send him home as soon as he tells them," Sarah said.

"Tells them what? That his wife is dying?"

"Matthias! She is not, she is only ill."

"She is dying. She knows, and so do we. So does Joseph. Ah, he is an old man so suddenly." Matthias could bear the gloom no longer. He hurried out the door yelling, "David ben Asher, are you outside? Let's go on a food hunt before the sun comes up and everyone else is awake. Maybe we can find a loose Roman horse in the Kidron Valley, or a dog in the city streets."

16

Titus stood on a huge boulder as the sun came up on the seventy-first day of the siege. Before him stood the Antonia mounted atop its rock shelf, which rested some seventy-five feet above the surrounding walled terrain. The fortress walls rose sixty more feet, and beyond this height her four corner towers loomed up even higher.

Titus perspired as he asked for a volunteer party to make the first assault with ladders while the rest of the Fifth Legion protected them with torrents of arrows. "The first man up the wall, if he lives," Titus let the words stand significantly alone, "I will make a centurion and a commander of those who are now his equals!"

Within seconds one named Sabinus, a lean veteran from Spoleto in central Italy, volunteered to be first and soon eleven others were racing with him bearing a ladder toward the Antonia's northern wall just moments before day began to break. The small band dug the foot of the ladder in place, and still undiscovered in the semidarkness, Sabinus began his climb to either fame or death.

"I'm sorry," said the wily old Zechariah, "but Simon has given the word. Every man stays and fights."

Joseph nodded, resigned himself to what he must do, and went to the edge of the wall and peered over. Suddenly he began to motion to Zechariah, saying, "Hurry! Come quickly!"

Zechariah's eyes bulged as he saw, in the quiet morning darkness, a lone Roman, a sword held in his mouth, climbing up a ladder directly beneath the two men on the wall. Instinctively Joseph pushed the ladder and the Roman broke the tranquil silence with a piercing scream as he fell to the jagged basalt rock below.

In seconds all was chaos. A thousand screams gave the alarm from the top of the Antonia wall as the awakened Jewish Zealots rained a storm of arrows on the daring morning intruders. From below the archers of the Fifth Legion sought to save their bravest men by hurling hundreds of arrows toward the guards atop the Antonia. Amid the arrows and burning torches flying in both directions, Titus could see his brave volunteer, an arrow through his chest. Titus shook his head in disbelief at the horror of this day which was yet so young.

Within minutes the arrows halted and the bodies were being dragged away. The Antonia in Zealot hands had held against the first of a dozen Roman onslaughts, but how long would it stand when thousands began to rush at it upon hundreds of ladders all being raised and climbed in the same moment?

With this first battle over, the soldiers paused for breakfast. The Romans were treated to hot wheat-and-barley cereal, while the starving Zealots ate crusts of stale bread and pieces of garbage, if they ate at all.

Three days later, on the seventy-third day, Joseph sat beside his wife, watching her grow weaker each moment. Zechariah had managed to obtain permission for Joseph to remain home for a day or two as a reward for giving the alarm.

Miriam was now delirious with the fever, which had reached plague proportions in the city. The lack of food, the strain, and the unsanitary conditions within Jerusalem had caught up with the dwindling population.

Old Uncle David was chanting somber prayers, rocking back and forth. Beside him sat Miriam's sixty-two-year-old mother, Rachel Zvi, weeping softly. Matthias and Sarah sat silently, waiting for Joseph to bring word from the sick-room.

At last he appeared. "She would like to speak to Uncle David," he announced.

The old man arose and went to the room slowly as the others watched him, their questions unspoken.

"Uncle David," Miriam murmured, "thank you for coming."

"Would I say no to you, child, who took figs from my hand before you could walk?" He smiled, and his heart nearly burst at the sight of her frailty. How small she had become! Even now, she seemed to be disappearing before his eyes. "Can I help you in some way?"

"I have spoken to my husband. He told me it would be best to tell you as well. Remember when I asked you to tell me more of Messiah and His coming?"

"I remember."

"I believe in Jesus of Nazareth, Uncle David. I have become a Christian."

His old heart beat faster, but he spoke calmly, kindly as ever. "What has made you believe, Miriam?"

"Many things—Alexandra, the teachings in the Temple." She stopped for a moment, obviously resting, gathering strength to continue.

"Miriam, you must not—"

"Why not? What can be lost? I will spend these last hours telling my family about my new love, and I shall die very happy."

"No, Miriam, of course you will not die."

"Dear Uncle, you know better. Please, listen to me. You are looking for Messiah. Uncle David, ask God for faith to believe. He will show you. Don't you see already? Messiah is the Promised One, but His Kingdom was not as we thought. The peace is here," she said and laid her hand

162

across her breast, "not out there in the city. Oh, Uncle David, my sins are upon Jesus. Do you understand?"

"I am trying, Miriam. I must be very sure. If you are sure—"

She nodded weakly, too tired to respond further.

"Then I am happy. The Lord will receive you at the resurrection, I know. I have prayed for you and I pray for myself, that I might know the truth and understand all that God has for me. I am yet learning. No doubt He has allowed you to be my teacher as well. Shall I tell your mother?"

Miriam shook her head. "She is not ready. She would be angry and troubled at my death. The others—wait." Her voice was barely a whisper, and David silently patted her hand and turned away.

He returned to the rest of the family. "She wanted prayer," he explained in partial truth to their questioning stares. "Rachel, perhaps you should go and watch with her."

By nightfall, the family was too numb to care when word came that the Antonia fortress had fallen to the Romans. Only Uncle David moaned, "Oh! Oh! Only the Temple cloister buildings remain to separate them from the courts."

The night wore on, and the sounds of war drifted on the crisp night air. Then, suddenly, a heartrending wail came from the room where Miriam lay.

Immediately Sarah covered her head with her arms and joined Rachel in lamenting the death of their daughter. Through the night, the mourning chant mingled with the cries of drunken soldiers and frightened civilians until dawn broke, bringing relief.

"These times," Rachel said bitterly as they returned from burying Miriam, "we must do everything quickly, without ceremony, even burying our dead. It is wrong."

"Perhaps. But we must not be away from the house long, either. We live, and we must try to continue," Matthais said, though he wondered.

Alone with Joseph, Uncle David asked, "You knew she was a Christian?"

"She told me some time ago."

"And you? Do you believe in Jesus also?"

"Ha! It seems to me that everyone connected with Jesus brings me sorrow. Alexandra, whom I loved, has gone. Miriam, whom I married, has died. He apparently cursed the city, so I am doomed to fight to the death in a war that is meaningless to me. But who was He to have such power? Does He hate me? Or is it the Almighty playing tricks?"

"Miriam was happy when she died. Christians believe that they will go to be with Jesus in heaven at the right hand of God."

"Uncle David, has the Scripture given you an answer? Is He the Messiah?"

Uncle David spoke cautiously. "From all that I know about Him, He could be the Messiah. I have found nothing in His life that is contrary to the Law and the prophets. But," he raised his arms, "still I doubt. Perhaps it is because I am old."

"But He defied the teaching of the rabbis. He dishonored the Sabbath and many other points of the Law."

"Not true, Joseph. Not the Law, but traditions. Ha! What are they? This war has made a mockery of tradition, of washing and right eating. The real Law, which was given to us by Moses, He never broke." Uncle David laughed out loud. "Listen to me defend the man! But Joseph, did you see Miriam? Can you deny that what she believed was real and good?"

Joseph shook his head. "She was certainly more righteous than I am. Like Leah, she loved me and served me when she knew I preferred another. And the bitterness and animosity she felt for Alexandra vanished. It could not have been only because we married and she felt secure. She changed, somehow."

"Do you believe, then?"

"No, Uncle David. I cannot. But do you?"

"Almost, Joseph. I believe that I almost believe. Yet I hesitate."

*   *   *

Joseph left his family, and the siege went on relentlessly. Eighty days, eighty-five, and then the Temple sacrifices ceased entirely. The starving people could no longer bring anything to sacrifice, and Roman arrows made it impossible for the priests to approach the great altar. Once again, the Jews lived without an offering for sin.

Ninety days, ninety-five, and the Romans began to break through to the Temple sanctuary. John of Gischala watched their progress and knew there would be no turning them back. He gave the signal to light the cloister buildings, considered sacred in themselves, so as to burn the leading Roman attackers alive. Previously positioned incendiary materials were lit in a score of locations and flames shot up simultaneously on every side at once, searing trapped Romans and overtaking them with instant terror.

The cries of pain were unbearable, even to the ears of those safe beyond. Many of the Roman soldiers attempted to race through the flames and jump to safety. If they tried that, they were dashed to death on the hard marble below both to the north and to the south of the cloisters. Those who ran east or west rushed into still more flames, fell off the roofs of buildings, or crashed into other men or objects in the smoke and fire.

The Zealots called to a Roman named Longus to come to them before the flames reached him. He fell on his own sword, not trusting the Zealots and fearing that they would torture him.

Still another soldier, Artorius, trapped on a burning roof, shouted to his tentmate, safe below, that if he would try to catch him he would give him everything he possessed. The one below agreed and Artorius jumped. The force of the one leaping for his life, however, crushed his brave companion against the stone pavement, killing him instantly. But Artorius lived.

The screams of pain, the awful sights of horror, and the unforgettable stench of men's flesh burning caused even General Titus to cast off his usual restraint.

He began shouting to those men whom he could see. "Jecundus," he called. "Stephanus! Your general thanks you! You are a tribute to Rome, and Rome will avenge!" He shouted louder, screamed, trying to stifle tears, until his voice broke, and then he turned his back on the holocaust and returned to his camp.

His stomach was uneasy, and he wanted only privacy, but as he rode past the interim prisoners' camp, he was impressed to see a group of people on their knees, watching the Temple cloisters burning. The people were also speaking softly into the warm wind.

"Centurion, what are these people doing?"

"I believe they are praying, General Titus."

"To what god?"

The soldier shrugged. "An invisible god, one I know little about. They are Christians."

Titus frowned. "Christianity has been unpopular in Rome, though I know little of it myself. Are these people unruly?"

"No. On the contrary, their conduct is exemplary. They pray for Romans as well as Jews, and they minister to the wounded in every possible way. They have even offered themselves as servants without being ordered to work. The women remain pure, and the soldiers do not take advantage of them because of their kindness. Many of them are Greeks

166

who came to worship at the annual Passover in Jerusalem, and were taken in with other Jewish prisoners."

"I must give them some consideration. There is no need to feed them if they might go free and support themselves in their home cities. There is certainly no need to keep them if they are no threat to us. Are there other colonies of them?"

"Yes, general, several. Some on each side of the city. Somehow they knew before the siege began that there would be trouble, and they left the city early, going in all directions."

"Where are you from? Do you know Christians at all?"

"I am from Caesarea. I have known a few."

"Go to all the interim camps. Select Christians from each area to represent their colonies. Make sure that there are some from many parts of the world. Bring the delegation to my tent. This war will soon be over. We might as well begin reassigning the prisoners now."

Before he reached his quarters, he was confronted by General Lepidus. "Sir, we found this old Jew trying to steal a horse."

"How far did he get?"

"He took the horse and was back into the valley when he was noticed. I don't know how he expected to regain entrance to the city. The gates are closed everywhere."

"He would have butchered the horse under cover of darkness and climbed the walls with the pieces. They have done it before." Titus was angry, thinking of the men still dying in the flames in the northwestern sector. "The soldier dies," he said sternly.

Lepidus stared at him, stunned. "For allowing his horse to be stolen?"

"Yes. I will not permit the Roman army to continue feeding the Jews so that they will prolong this siege for more months. One horse can feed a hundred Zealots for days.

Then they can hold out for another week beyond that, and during that same time, perhaps five hundred more Jewish civilians starve, and perhaps another fifty Romans are killed by Jewish arrows from the walls. It has been the policy all along. Don't ask for exceptions now. We *will* stop this carelessness on the part of our men with their horses. Execute him at once, and the thief as well."

Titus rode off with his aide. General Lepidus gave a shrug of his shoulders, then made a motion with his hand to a centurion, who silently ordered the sentence of Titus to be carried out. Lepidus spun and walked swiftly to his tent, rage and pity mingling within. A Roman, a man of his own elite Tenth Legion, would die, not in battle, but on a humiliating, ghastly cross. For the aging Jew he had no sympathy.

"Crucify him," came the icy words of the red-bearded young centurion as he pointed to Uncle David. The ugly words fell on ears that knew no Latin, and Uncle David, confused, afraid, was pushed along to the edge of the camp. Minutes later he saw the cross, and his stomach heaved as the full realization of his situation overwhelmed him. The once-powerful giant, now weakened from lack of food, had his hands and feet nailed to a cross already stained red from the blood of previous victims. Uncle David was in utter loneliness here on what was once an attractive, flower-covered Jerusalem hillside just outside the East, or "Beautiful," Gate. Guttural noises of infinite agony escaped from his lips as the pain radiated through his body.

Lifted up for all the camp to see, Uncle David allowed his head to fall forward, shamed beyond imagination.

It had seemed the thing to do. They were all so hungry. From the wall they could see the well-fed animals roaming about. The sight was too tantalizing! David was a good rider. He knew that he could capture a horse if he could reach the shelter of the valley and wait for nightfall. But he had not reckoned on the weakness of his body or the strength of the soldiers. He had failed. The day passed, time measured by the old man in searing encounters with pain. But his thoughts were racing. He was dying. There could be no question about that. He must decide *now* whether Jesus of Nazareth was the Messiah. For a moment he thought of that man alone, like himself, on a cross, a victim of Roman oppression.

A pain that was more than physical stabbed at him. The Romans had not killed Jesus by themselves. He remembered his father's account of the trial. *"We will not have him over us. . . . We have no king but Caesar."* But what *would have happened if he had been lauded and hailed and given the position as King, Lord of the Sabbath? He was above and beyond the Law, truer than tradition, and, yes,* David had to admit to himself, *more righteous than the Pharisees.*

Through the day, Uncle David weighed, balanced, and sorted what he knew of Jesus of Nazareth. The life seeped out of his body as he pieced together the gossip, the Scripture, the facts about the life of the Nazarene. *No more time,* his pounding heart seemed to tell him. He must declare allegiance to the God of his fathers and their way of life, or to a Galilean who interrupted his solid order so late in time.

"Son of man, the righteous branch, the root of Jesse.* Jehovah God and Jesus of Nazareth seemed to stand before him, two figures far away on the city wall, calling. Then, as the perspiration rolled into his eyes, they became one. David winked his eyes, and even that tiny movement was infinitely painful. Two, or one?

"Of course," he murmured. That had been the cause of all the trouble. "You make yourself God," they had accused, "when you are only a man."† Of course He was a

*See Isaiah 11 and Matthew 26:63-64.
†See John 10:30-33.

man. But was He a prophet of God? That had been David's question until this moment, when suddenly he realized the real issue. Was He not only a prophet, but truly God, an incarnation of the infinite Jehovah? *Lord of the Sabbath, Son of God.* He squinted into the distance. The sky was now streaked with pink and gray, and the glow from the burning temple cloisters settled and dimmed. He saw no figures on the city wall.

Then, like a ghost, the pleasant face of Alexandra, the Greek girl who had taken shelter in his home, came before him. She was closer than the other figures, and she seemed concerned, even upset, and her look of love stirred his failing heart.

You cared for us, he thought. *You, with your foreign ways, coming to worship our God in your strange new way. But how you listened and learned, and held your tongue when Sarah, that old camel, was rude to you. You know so much of God, and I have missed so much.* And while the face dimmed and darkened, he uttered, in agony, his decision.

"You are the Christ, the Son of God, Redeemer of Israel. Receive me, for I believe." And there fell to the earth, trampled by Roman soldiers, the final expression of David ben Asher's life—two tears, one of regret, the other of joy.

17

Alexandra watched him die, tears pouring down her cheeks, aware that he was too near death to recognize or talk with her. In a moment she was joined by other Christians answering a summons to congregate at the edge of the camp.

"Uncle David," she whispered to a friend. "I wonder about the others." She moved along with the men and women in her group, sick at heart and preoccupied with the scene of the dear old man on the cross.

"We may be released," she heard. "Titus is sending for us. We must pray for guidance when the selections are made."

They joined other small groups of Christians and were assembled in order by the soldiers. A centurion came riding toward them, then stopped and dismounted.

"Are there any here from Caesarea?" he asked.

"I am," Alexandria responded softly. Her thoughts suddenly turned in a new direction at the sound of the soldier's question.

He turned in the direction of the voice, his eyes going up and down the row of faces until he located Alexandra.

"Yes," she said. "It is I, Alexandra. Were you looking for me, Thaddeus?"

Thaddeus laughed—a happy, bright laugh—and tossed his helmet high.

"Alexandra! I've found you!"

The other Christians mumbled happily, speculating, while Alexandra stepped forward.

"Come over here. Let me look at you," he said. "I never

really thought I would see you again! Titus sent me on this mission, and I knew it would be the best chance to find you, if you were here at all." He grinned his expansive grin. "I've won again, against all odds."

Thaddeus selected other Christians from other cities to join him, and they returned to the area of Titus' headquarters. Along the way, he told Alexandra about his coming into Titus' command and his duties during the siege. She told him of the Matthias household, her stay in Jerusalem, and the death of Uncle David.

"If only I had known! We could surely have obtained clemency. I am so sorry."

"He is in God's hands," she said.

"And you, are you still so sure of your religion?"

She smiled, happy in spite of her circumstances, and said nothing.

"Naturally you are. It's like you. Just wait till we get back to Caesarea. I'll persuade you to marry me yet. I shall receive a promotion after the siege. We can have a home."

Her continued silence told him her answer had not changed, but Thaddeus was undaunted. "I shall always love you, Alexandra, even when you look as terrible as you look now. Give me time. I *never* lose."

The next day, on the other side of the camp, General Titus, mighty in battle, melted like snow when he realized who was entering his tent.

"Tell this guard to let me in," came the soft, lilting voice of Queen Bernice. Her red curls hung softly from her highly set coiffure, and they fell gently over her one bare shoulder. She was dressed in a green robe bedecked with woven yellow strands. Her luxurious beauty stood in sharp contrast to the gaunt faces of her fellow Jews, long ago hollowed and colorless. And her ultimate femininity stood in sharp relief against the thousands of men in the military camp.

"Good morning. Have you come for breakfast?" he could not yet be relaxed in her presence, though she had been with him for weeks. He busied himself with collecting his personal articles.

"Titus, stop that. I really must speak to you."

He went to her boldly and kissed her to settle himself. "Now," he said. "What is so important that you rise this early?"

"Titus, don't tease me now. I am very serious. Ten days ago your men burned down the northern cloisters and porticos, which surround the great Temple court. Today your machines are beating the western wall of the Inner Temple itself! They say that you will break through within hours. I beg of you, please save our Temple, the holy sanctuary building itself." His strange look of confusion and disbelief urged her on. "Please, Titus! For me. Save the Temple, and God will bless you for it."

Titus paused, caught off guard. He tried to think quickly, to guess her motives.

"Why is the Temple so important to you?"

"I am a Jew! It is my Temple, the house of my God. Have you no beliefs at all?" She was irritated, and it made Titus quick to answer.

"I only wanted to hear your ideas. I do not understand, really, but of course I will do what I can—for you." She seemed relieved, and as his thoughts caught up with him, he added, "You realize that I have needs as well."

"I see. And what is it you ask in return?" Her voice softened, and he continued, knowing that she was receptive.

"The siege will soon be over. We shall all return to Rome. My father is the emperor, you know," he said lightly. "I will have a great deal to do in Rome. You would enjoy Rome, if you were to come with me."

She was quiet. She had not expected this response from him. She walked about the tent humming, thinking, then said, "What will you do with the Christians?"

"I have not decided. Do you have a request about them as well?"

She wrinkled her nose. "They are fools. I once heard a great leader among them, one called Paul the apostle."

"What did he say to you?"

"Nothing. He ignored me."

"Then he was most certainly blind," Titus said, and drew her close to himself.

"The Temple?" she asked.

"Rome?" said Titus.

She gave a slight nod, and he quickly left her to send orders to the city that the Temple should be spared.

By the next day, the ninth of Av (July-August), the one hundred seventh day of the siege, the fires both the Jews and the Romans had set the previous night in the buildings around the Temple were still smouldering. The Romans had set them to destroy; the Zealots had ignited them to keep Roman swordsmen at bay. Both sides awaited the lifting of the final curtain of smoke.

At midday some of the Zealots clashed bitterly with Romans, but the full force of neither side was felt. The battle actually occurred between what might be called the fire control personnel of each side. Nevertheless, Joseph and Zechariah were content to watch from the distant Inner-Temple walls as two small groups cut each other down with a fury.

By sundown both Joseph and Zechariah, like most of the Romans, were sitting and resting, having been alerted that it was Titus' plan to storm the Temple the next morning. But a daring Roman soldier, no doubt thinking that

174

he was performing an act which would make him a hero, persuaded another to sneak up with him in the dimming twilight to the northern edge of the Temple building. While his companion hoisted him up, he silently laid a torch on a wooden windowsill of the sanctuary, even as priestly prayers could be heard from within. Within seconds the lavish inlaid wood within the window caught fire, and suddenly, without warning, the whole interior was ablaze. The huge wooden beams within, which held up the walls and supported the roof, quickly caught the flames. Thus two soldiers, apparently acting on their own, brought down the Temple of an entire nation and of that nation's God.

Titus could barely contain his rage, and he at once issued an order to his chief centurion to quench the fire, but it was too late. Both Jewish and Roman fire fighters were driven back as the Temple burned out of control. The hand-to-hand fighting with swords was fanatical on both sides. All the while smoke prevented leaders on both sides from seeing their own men, let alone controlling them. The shoutings of the sword-slashing Romans, now tasting ultimate victory, combined with the pitiful wailing of the frenzied, knife-wielding, self-sacrificing Jewish defenders. The falling Temple stones, the path of the fire, the hot smoke, and the noise of battle created an indescribable chaos of blood, fire, and agony.

Titus wheeled his beautiful stallion and raced to his tent, hoping to reach Bernice before the news of the fire reached her. He ran to her, breathless, just as she was about to leave.

"Bernice—"

"I see you changed your mind," she said coldly.

"No, please, I ordered my men to save the Temple. It was a mistake!"

"Oh. I see. And you still want me in Rome, then?"

His relief was unbounded. "Yes! Yes!"

"I shall be going. King Herod has been honored for his contribution to the war, and will live in Rome henceforth. I am his queen, after all."

She left him there, gasping with rage and humiliation, alone with his imminent victory. The Romans would hail him upon his return, and even build a monument bearing the image of the Temple menorah, but would Bernice ride beside him through the conqueror's arch?

18

The unexpected burning of the Temple played havoc with military strategy. Among the Zealot forces, it was every man for himself.

"Throw away your bow and arrows, Joseph. The Romans are too close. Use your sword," shouted Zechariah to his younger comrade.

"I've said a prayer for you, Zechariah!"

"Die valiantly, Joseph. Here they come!"

The wild, shouting, sword-brandishing Roman foot soldiers approached in line after line, swords pointed ahead. Smoke blinded everyone's eyes and many men tripped over debris, often feeling in an instant the iron of the sword. Joseph and Zechariah, being inexperienced in such combat, gave ground and began to run southward as the Romans started to regroup. As the Temple burned on, its flames now lighting the darkening sky, the Romans commenced all the more to cheer and shout. Victory was at last theirs and they became unstoppable.

Joseph gave an involuntary cry of horror and grief as he saw Zechariah fall upon a marble pavement block in the court of the Gentiles. Within a second of the slip a pursuing Roman stabbed Zechariah through the stomach with his short, black, two-edged iron sword. It happened only five yards behind Joseph, and he could do nothing but race with those around him toward the temporary protection of the south cloister buildings. They alone stood between the burning sanctuary and the safety of the Hulda Gates, which led to "David's City"—the oldest section of the city—which was still in Jewish hands.

For minutes, although it seemed to be an hour, Joseph was unable to get to the Hulda Triple Gate, named for its three doorways. If the fleeing Zealots locked the gates before he got through, he would be trapped in the south cloister buildings until the advancing Roman mobs reached him.

Suddenly he felt himself knocked down. His mouth struck a stone, a tooth broke, his mouth and chin were cut and he began to bleed. He lost his sword, but did not waste time hunting for it as he arose. He groped among the white limestone pillars of the Royal Portico as throngs of fleeing Zealots pushed along with him. Periodically a heroic Zealot would push by him going the other way with either a drawn sword or a flaming torch. Joseph knew that he himself was no match for the Romans. Perspiring both from the heat of the Temple flames and the fear of his imminent death, he pressed on, step by step, blood now flowing from his mouth, toward the Hulda Gates and safety in the City of David and the south half of Jerusalem. All around him were wailing Zealots, bemoaning their own wounds, their fallen comrades, and the devastation of their Temple by Gentile pagans.

At the sight of the first of the three Hulda Gates Joseph's heart stopped—it was already closed! He pushed on amid the throng, pulling, shoving, groping, until with pounding heart he reached the second gate.

"No more, no more," shouted a Zealot guard desperately trying to push the heavy wooden gate closed while hitting with a wooden pole the people who were still shoving to gain entrance. "We must close the gate." The huge, bearded fellow gave Joseph a poke in his midsection with the wooden pole, knocking his breath away. He struggled on, borne along with the crowd, to the third door. It was open, but hands behind were pushing, pushing relentlessly. Joseph reached out over heads, and thrust in his hand and forearm. The door pinched him, and he yelled and pushed harder, smothering those below him. The door opened an inch, six inches. He was inside! The door slammed shut behind him amid screams of the hopeless on the other side.

Joseph cried like a child, tears running down his cheek, mixing with the blood. He followed the crowd southward into the Ophel Hill and the Davidic ancient city. What had happened to his city?

*"The joy of the whole earth, is mount Zion, . . . the city of the great King. God is known in her palaces for a refuge. . . . God will establish it for ever. . . . Tell the towers thereof. Mark ye well her bulwarks, . . . that ye may tell it to the generation following."** The Scripture seemed a mockery to Joseph as he looked out over the burning debris, and another of David's writings worked through his memory to express his own feelings. "O LORD God, to whom vengeance belongeth," he cried to the smoky heavens, "shew thyself. . . . How long shalt the wicked triumph? How long shall they utter and speak hard things? and all the workers of iniquity boast themselves?" The sorrow of defeat overwhelmed him. He shouted, "They break in pieces thy people, O LORD, and afflict thine heritage." He walked, sniffling like a lost child, with people rushing past him on all sides, trying to find comfort in the promise that followed the question. "The LORD will not cast off his people, neither will he forsake his inheritance."†

Joseph had not realized his love for this, his city, until he saw it ruined. Going up to his father's house, he saw the places where he had played in childhood, the familiar wells, the marketplaces, the houses of friends, some burning already.

He walked along, searching for friendly faces. Finding none, he settled for a doorway in which to sleep a few hours.

*Psalm 48:2-3, 8, 12-13.
†Psalm 94:1, 3-5, 14.

The misery of the Hebrews, the desperation of the continued vain self-sacrifices of the Zealots and Sicarii, and the pandemonium of the Romans set this night, the ninth of Av, apart from all other nights as a night of horror. For centuries to come, Jewish couples about to be wed would remember this night by breaking a glass moments before exchanging their final marriage vows. They would do this, amid their supreme moment of happiness, to recall publicly for an instant the tragedy, the despair, and the utter impossibility of ever again mending the broken Temple.

And likewise, for the years beyond, pilgrims and wayfarers from out of every tribe of the Jewish nation would, if fortunate enough to reach Jerusalem in their lifetime, stand by the stones of the western wall to weep and wail in mourning for the Temple, which once stood nearby.

As the next day arrived, the Romans began to bring their ensigns—idolatrous eagle standards, like flags—into the Temple mount while the burning embers of the sanctuary still smoked in unabated fury. As soldiers drank to Bacchus, god of wine, others danced about, shaking their metal eagles and plaques bearing the letters S.P.Q.R. (*Senatus Populus Que Romanus*—"The Senate and People which is Rome"). The battle was nearly over.

Joseph arrived at his boyhood house to find his parents missing and the house occupied by refugees. He passed the following days of siege looking for them, posing as a follower of the Zealots. He was waiting for the end to come, wondering what would happen to him when the Romans finally finished here. It was rumored that Titus had given word that no one should be killed unless he resisted, but what did that mean to Joseph? He would gladly have surrendered and ended the suspense, except that Simon's men would have killed him instantly.

Throughout the month of the upper-city siege, he was troubled by thoughts of Alexandra. He wished he could forget the shape of her face and the tone of her voice, and think more of Miriam. He felt guilty and at the same time angry because Alexandra was gone, safe in Caesarea with her family, while he sat here waiting for his uncertain fate to catch up with him.

But perhaps the worst part was that he could never separate thoughts of Alexandra from her ideas about Jesus of Nazareth. He wondered how he could have loved this woman so deeply and yet rejected her faith. It was so much a part of her, and, according to her own claims, it made her the person she was. She had known all along that this destruction would happen. She had told all of them, but they had not believed her. *It was easy for her,* he argued with himself, *to accept the Nazarene's claims. She had not been raised in Jerusalem, in the shadow of the Temple, seeing the smoke rise each morning and evening, celebrating the Sabbath and the special feasts, believing that sins were covered by sacrifice.*

That was the difference, she had told him. Sins were covered by sacrifice, but in the Christ, sin was removed, done away with completely, remembered no more by the Father. And it was true that she did believe that Jehovah was one God.

Joseph fantasized, imagining himself a Christian, and tried to sense how it would feel. He explored many possibilities in those days, the last of the siege. He thought of the teaching he had received in the synagogue and in the schools as a young boy. And he questioned whether Jesus could truly be the Messiah of Israel.

Gradually, day after day, with little else to occupy his thoughts, he began to understand the love that filled Alexandra's heart. He realized, as he saw the Romans triumphant on every side, that being chosen of God meant more than the kind of supremacy he had known in his lifetime.

He regretted the years he had spent vying for positions

of favor with Rome. The favor and possessions which had followed were nothing now. In the end, he was alone before God. What had he accumulated in his life to offer the Holy One?

He wanted to belong to God in a deeper, more lasting way. The death he witnessed, the death he inflicted, the death he narrowly escaped, made him think of the grave—and beyond—as never before. If what Alexandra told him was true, that Jesus died and lived again, then the Nazarene was the key, the way through which he might find God in a personal way.

Though he avoided combat as much as possible, he carried a short sword with which to defend himself. While circling a house one day he chanced upon a lone Roman looking for the other members of his unit.

"Halt!" cried the Roman. "Whom do you serve?"

Joseph hesitated. What should be his reply? At last he answered, truthfully, "None but myself."

The Roman peered quizzically at him, his sword at Joseph's belly, then smiled. "A happy and fortunate man, no doubt."

"Not at the moment," Joseph said, arms wide apart. The Roman reached for Joseph's sword, and as he did so, Joseph noticed a small crescent drawn in the sand. It was a sign Alexandra had shown him, a sign among Christians. Carefully he stepped forward and completed the sign by drawing another crescent joined to the first to form the fish, the Greek *ichthyus,* the sign of the Christ.

"You? A Christian?" asked the soldier.

Joseph shook his head. "A seeker. Are you a Christian?"

He nodded. "You are a man with no masters, and I have many, Jesus the Christ being the best. What keeps you from believing?"

Still they stood, the Roman's sword now lowered. Joseph replied, "I am a Jew."

182

"As He was. Do not let the fact that God deals with you in special ways keep you from Him. Jesus was sent for you, His people, first—and to us second."

"So I am told by others of you. But—I am torn."

The soldier nodded. "As you say, you are a man with no masters. Is it because you loathe being a servant?"

Like lightning the truth about himself came to Joseph. It seemed as if the naming of his pride flew from the man's sword directly into his heart. It was true. He had chosen friendship with Rome rather than being her subject. He was happy to be a Jew, favored of Jehovah, but he could not bear the idea of sacrifice and service. He could not even declare loyalty to any war factions because he felt that the leaders were all inferior to himself. A man with no master indeed! His own pride held him in chains.

And Jesus? Could Joseph now humble himself to choose a way illustrated by women and soldiers? Could he claim love for one whom he had openly scorned?

The longings of his heart brought on by war would not go unsatisfied. He stood silently before the soldier as his heart cried inwardly, *Lord, I believe. Make me Your own.*

At the point of desperation he willingly gave his life into the keeping of Jesus, whom he now called the Christ. As he marched away to the Roman camp, he dreamed of the Kingdom that was yet to come and he rejoiced in the peace that filled his heart. His one regret was that he could not talk about his joy with Miriam—or with Alexandra.

19

The lines of people were crooked and broken, as ragged and forlorn as the people of which they were composed. Roman centurions walked along, inspecting, choosing the strong ones for service in the mines of Egypt and the ships of Rome, the weak ones to be marched until they died on the way to Rome—and some to go to Caesarea to fight against each other in the gladiatorial rings. Like animals, they were herded, rerouted, positioned, ordered, but at least, Joseph thought, not killed. Constantly he watched for some sign of his parents or uncle, until at last he was designated as a mine worker and placed with another group composed of strong young men.

Food was brought to them. For many of them it was the first real food they had had in weeks—good bread, clean water, even fruit. They began to speak to each other, and then someone laughed. Relief spread through the group until every man there felt at ease again, just being alive.

Joseph was speaking to another man, debating how they would be transported, and did not notice the centurion who walked past with a young woman beside him. She looked closely at the men and listened. She walked on, then returned, listened again, and came and stood respectfully at Joseph's elbow.

"Joseph? It is Joseph!"

In a moment they were tight in each other's arms, laughing, shouting, death swallowed up in life, the lost found.

"Thaddeus, this is Joseph! This is Joseph, of the house of Matthias. We have found him, do you see?"

Thaddeus scratched his ear and looked on, head tilted,

a half-smile on his face. "I certainly do see. This is your friend, did you say?"

Alexandra drew back, suddenly self-conscious. "Yes, yes. Joseph, where are your mother and father and Miriam?"

"Miriam is dead of the fever. My mother and father are gone, I do not know where, nor did I find Uncle David."

She shook her head. "They are all gone, then. I have looked everywhere, in all the prisoner camps. Only these few men are left. Your parents are not here, and Uncle David—I know he is dead."

"But you!" said Joseph. "I can't believe it. You are here! Why?"

"I have been here throughout the siege. I was taken just two days after I left the city, for the armies were just arriving as we went north. We had traveled slowly, meeting other groups leaving the city and trying to warn those we met going in, and we walked right into the advance guard. Most of the other Christians are gone now, but Titus himself gave me permission to stay and look for you and your family. Joseph, this is my friend Thaddeus from Caesarea. We were good friends before the war. He has helped me a great deal."

"And you are my friend, too," Thaddeus declared. "Joseph, where are they sending you?"

"To Egypt, to the mines." The joy of the moment vanished, and in the solemn quiet, Joseph thought of still more news. "Alexandra, I believe. And so did Miriam, and perhaps Uncle David as well. You have changed our lives forever."

Then she began to cry, and Thaddeus and Joseph watched her leave for her own tent, not understanding. The two men told each other about their experiences for a time, and in only a short while they felt that they were friends. Joseph marveled at his position—a Christian,

185

speaking freely with Romans, and as he looked out into the night sky, he knew that he was still hopelessly in love with a Greek.

In the morning, they would begin the grueling overland march toward Egypt, and he would be a prisoner, not unlike his great ancestor Joseph. Would God prosper him, as he had that other man so long ago? Would Israel again emerge as a great nation? He wondered.

Thaddeus appeared at the tent of general Titus early the next day.

"What do you wish, centurion?"

"Clemency, general, for one of the Jerusalem prisoners."

"Male?"

"Yes, but not a resister, nor a key leader. An ordinary soldier."

Titus was skeptical. "If ordinary, why do you plead for him?"

"He is a friend, and the friend of a friend."

Titus shook his head. "It would be too difficult. Favoritism in such matters always causes trouble. Besides, where would he go?"

"With his friend, to Caesarea no doubt. He is Christian. I am sure he would cause no trouble."

"I'm afraid not."

Thaddeus drew a coin from a small purse at his waist. "Do you enjoy a game, General?"

"On occasion."

"Would this not be an occasion? You are a great winner, sir. The gods are obviously with you. Let me ask that with the toss of the coin, we decide the destination of the prisoner. Heads, to Egypt. Tails, to Caesarea."

Titus paused, then smiled and nodded. "I like your spirit, Thaddeus. And yes, in some ways, I am a winner. Toss the coin."

Thaddeus flipped the coin up toward the tent ceiling, caught it deftly, and with more apprehension than he cared to show, opened his palm. Titus walked over to inspect the coin: "Hmph! So the prisoner is lucky too. Send him to Caesarea then, as a free man. Go now. I have business to attend to. Enough of games."

Before the sun came up the next morning Alexandra was saying good-bye to Joseph. "You are not bitter?" she asked him.

He only shook his head. "I have seen you alive and well. And I have hope. We Jews have a reputation for surviving. Who can tell what will happen tomorrow?"

She trembled visibly and bit her lip. "I can't help it," she said. "I am so sad, when I should be happy. Oh, Joseph, I feel like Naomi. The Lord has taken everything I have!"

"He gave to Naomi children in her old age. Can you wait for me?"

She nodded, unable to speak. The rustlings about them reminded them that the march was only minutes away. There was nothing more to say.

She pressed his hand, turned, and walked away as Thaddeus came to meet her.

"Alexandra, I have news."

She brightened a little. "Of Matthias and Sarah?"

He shook his head. "I'll be returning to Caesarea soon. Will you marry me?"

"Are you a Christian?" she asked in her usual friendly tone.

"What if I say that I am?"

"Oh, Thaddeus, are you?"

He looked away, unable to lie to her. "Not today. But what if I were? Would you marry me then?"

She took his hand. "If only I could love you, Thaddeus! We are such good friends. Why do you suppose I can feel nothing else for you?"

"I suppose it is because you are so in love already with Joseph."

They watched the columns of men form and begin to walk toward Egypt. Joseph turned and raised a hand, and Alexandra waved back. Thaddeus knew that, for the moment, he was forgotten.

"Thaddeus," Alexandra whispered, her voice tight with tears, "do men ever come out of Egypt?"

"Sometimes. Will you still love him when he is sixty-nine?"

"Oh, Thaddeus, don't joke."

"Alexandra, you won't marry me, ever?"

"I'm afraid not."

He sighed. "I thought so. Well, you can marry Joseph. He is a free man. I went to Titus and asked for his freedom."

"You did what?"

"I won his freedom in a coin toss. Now go and tell him before he gets to Egypt."

"What? I—what have you done? I don't understand!"

"Here!" He thrust the papyrus with Titus' seal on it into her hand. "It's the authorization of Titus, and the money is from me—a wedding present in advance, since I won't be coming."

Speechless, she stared at the writing and the money, and did not move.

Thaddeus laughed. "Where are your feet? Get going!" He turned her around and made her walk, and then she began to run, catching up with the guard in only a moment, waving the paper under his nose.

Thaddeus mumbled, "I never—well, hardly ever—lose."

Joseph, in the tradition of his fathers, broke into song. And together they sang a new song unto the Lord.

"Happy is he that hath the God of Jacob for his help,

whose hope is in the LORD his God: . . . The LORD looseth
the prisoners: The LORD openeth the eyes of the blind: the
LORD raiseth them that are bowed down. . . . Praise ye the
LORD."*

*Psalm 146:5, 7-8, 10.

EPILOGUE

After a total of 139 days of siege, the city of Jerusalem fell entirely into Roman hands. The two leaders of the revolt, John of Gischala and Simon ben Giora, were captured. John was condemned to perpetual imprisonment, while Simon was marched with the captives to Rome. At the end of the triumphal procession for Vespasian and Titus, Simon was butchered, as was the customary fate of the captive enemy general of highest rank.

The surviving captives of Jerusalem, almost a hundred thousand, it is estimated, were in the main marched in chains to Rome as prisoners. On the march to Rome, some twenty-five hundred Jewish prisoners were set against each other in Caesarea in gladiatorial contests, so the horrors were far from ended even with the fall of the city.

The Arch of Triumph of Titus, today near the Colosseum, was erected about A.D. 85 to commemorate this captivity, and still today an etching of the Temple menorah can be seen on its stone facing.